The Lamb

Third Book of The Birthright Series

by

Jacci Turner

 Lucky Bat Books

The Lamb
The Third Book in The Birthright Series
Copyright 2012 , Jacci Turner
Cover Artist: Tatiana Fernandez

10-9-8-7-6-5-4-3-2-1

ISBN: 978-1-939051-11-0
Published by Lucky Bat Books
LuckyBatBooks.com

Discover other titles by this author at JacciTurner.com.

DEDICATION

To Micah, my sweet boy who is now a grown man. I love
that you won't pass by without hugging me. Nobody can make
me laugh like you do. Thank you for your love and support
from Army bases around the world. I am proud of you for
standing up for you convictions.

Love, Mom

CONTENTS

The Lamb

Third Book of The Birthright Series

by

Jacci Turner

small window on the left side of the house. A bathroom window? Why did he feel drawn to it? Was there something he was supposed to do? He stood and tried to figure out why he'd been brought here. That's how he thought of it: brought here.

I guess I should go in. Then he noticed a low fence by his knees, a white picket fence, around the yard. *A white picket fence? Maybe this is just a dream.* He smiled at the thought. Why was he joking with himself in a dream? This was serious; he needed to concentrate.

He pushed open the low gate and walked slowly up the cracked cement path that divided the yard in two. With each step, his dread increased. His heart became a hammer in his chest.

He paused in front of the covered porch and stared at the peeling white paint on the front door. Should he go in?

A scream pierced the air. Ty's heart squeezed painfully against his ribcage and his breath caught in his throat.

He sat bolt upright in bed.

Ty glanced around his room, panting. He felt shaky and disoriented. He scanned the familiar shelves full of science trophies and the college brochures stacked on his bedside table. His feet were warm. He could smell dirty socks and the pepperoni from last night's snack. He forced himself to breathe more slowly. His chest relaxed.

He ran his hands over his short hair. No, not again. Last summer was bad enough. He'd had dreams like this during his time in summer school. They grew in detail, strength, and frequency until he was so exhausted he could barely see straight. *I can't afford to deal with this right now. Not now!*

He had honors classes to worry about. He had to keep his grades up for college. And college, that was another problem altogether; he would have to make a decision about it soon.

But then ... the past dreams like this had led to saving Dawna from sex traffickers. Was something like that happening again? His left eye began to twitch and he pressed his fingers into it. He thought back to this new strange dream. He felt the intense dread that came with it and shivered.

Ty glanced at his phone on the nightstand. Three a.m. *Damn!* He couldn't even call Lando. Well, he could call. Lando would want him to call. But to wake him up and say, "Hey, I had a dream about a white house. It was really scary," how lame was that? No, he needed to go back to sleep. Only three hours until the alarm went off for school. He would tell Lando tomorrow. Lando was pretty much his best friend, which was odd since they'd known each other less than a year. But Lando would want to know about the dream. He'd been through this with Ty the first time.

The person he really wanted to call was Tiff. He'd met Tiff and Lando in the same summer school class, along with Lando's girl-friend, Sammy. Just the sound of Tiff's voice would be reassuring. He could hear her laugh and say, "A scary white house? Whatever, Ty." He smiled at the thought of the cute dimple on her cheek that appeared when she laughed.

Then he rolled back over to bury his face in his pillow and pound his mattress with this fist. "Damn!" Tiff was just one more problem he had no answer for. He couldn't call her because he'd been pretty much banned from her life. Her folks had seen to that.

Tiff, schoolwork, choosing a college, and now this dream ... how was he ever going to get back to sleep?

$\sim$

TY SAT IN HIS OLD SUBARU STATION wagon in front of Wooster High School. He waited for Lando. A cold January wind blasted his car. His last class got out before Lando's, so Ty had driven across town to intercept his friend. He'd done this before, a couple of times since his break-up with Sheila. He'd felt the need to get away from his school and be with someone who understood him. It seemed like the whole school was mad at him for breaking up with Sheila, like they were the perfect couple and he'd ruined it. But he didn't feel about Sheila the way he felt about Tiff. Once he realized that, there was no reason to go on pretending.

Students began to file out of the rectangular, red-and-white-brick buildings, and Ty scanned the crowds. Lando was short and stocky, but Ty could pick him out easily because of his walk. It was bouncy, like he was always happy, which Lando pretty much was. Sure enough, he soon saw Lando's head as it popped up and down through the crowd, a mile-wide smile on his face. Ty tapped his horn to let Lando know he was in the parking lot. Lando recognized their signal and turned to find Ty. He waved goodbye to his friends and headed to the car. Ty rolled down the passenger window and Lando stuck his head in.

"Hey, Lando," Ty called.

"Hey, Ty, what's up?"

"No debate team today?"

"Nope."

"Have time for Megabucks? I'll buy."

"I was gonna take the bus over to Sammy's."

"I'll give you a ride."

"You sure?"

"Sure. It's on my way."

"Then I've got time! You know I love me some Starbucks." Lando pulled open the door and tossed his backpack into the back. Cold air rushed in with him.

Belted in, Lando glanced at Ty, then looked again. "You okay, man?"

Ty smiled. Lando knew how to read him all right. "I had a dream last night."

Lando jerked his head to flip his black hair out of his eyes. "Uh-oh ... what kind of dream?"

"Well," Ty began as he slowly drove his car from the parking lot along with hundreds of other students. "The Dawna kind."

"No way."

"Yep, only this time I was just standing in front of a white house. Just standing there and feeling intense ... dread."

"Dread?"

"Yeah. It was creepy."

Lando glanced at him with wrinkles of concern on his forehead, "So ... no girls to be rescued, no trucks, or anyone running like last time—just a house?"

"Yep. Just a house. Then I decided to go in, and when I got to the porch, there was a freaking loud scream."

"No way!" Lando zipped up his coat as if he'd felt a chill. "That's freaky, dude."

"You got it."

"Anything else?"

"No, I woke up."

Lando sat, quiet. "Was it a girl's scream? You know, as opposed to a boy or a baby or a man ..."

That's what Ty liked about Lando. He didn't have to explain himself, because he knew Lando believed him and wanted to help. Ty considered his question.

"It was definitely female, not like a guy or an old person, and not like a kid."

"Dang."

"Yep."

"Ty, do you think it's happening again? You know, like what happened with Dawna?"

"I was hoping you'd know, man."

Lando shook his head. "Maybe it was just bad pastrami."

Ty laughed. "I actually ate pizza right before bed. Maybe that's it."

"I hope that's it, man."

"Me too."

CHAPTER TWO
TIFF

Tiff smashed a serve over the net of the indoor court and Lorna lunged for it. Lorna's strawberry blonde hair flew out behind her as she dived to return the serve, but missed.

"Yes!" Tiff said and jumped into the air. "Game over!" She had beaten Lorna for the first time ever. Her game was definitely improving.

"Great game," said Lorna with typical good sportsmanship. They met at the net to shake hands. Even though it was Saturday and they were just playing for fun, they always observed the etiquette of the game.

Tiff couldn't stop her grin and had to rub it in as she danced around, chanting in a sing-song voice, "I beat you, I beat you! Even on your home court, I beat you!"

"Well, I wouldn't call the Grand Sierra Resort my home court. I don't live in a casino."

"You might as well; you're here all the time."

"True, but only 'cause my dad gives me privs. Hey, speaking of that, wanna go bowling after this? Or take in a movie?

Tiff was disappointed but she couldn't go. Lorna had no idea what it was like to be a Korean American. She was kept on a short leash. Although Tiff knew her parents loved and supported her, she also wished for more freedom.

Lorna had moved to Reno in November and planned to join the tennis team in the spring. Tiff's coach at Reno High introduced her to Tiff and they had been practice partners ever since. Tiff was thrilled to meet someone who had free access to indoor courts. Winter in Reno could be brutal and Tiff hated nothing more than being locked inside all winter with no tennis. Tiff was just getting to know Lorna and she rarely got to hang out with her outside of school or practice. She realized Lorna still waited for an answer.

"I wish I could, but my mom will pick me up in twenty minutes."

"Well, it's enough time to go grab an ice cream cone, anyway."

"Awesome."

That's what Tiff liked about Lorna; she never took anything personally, and she was easygoing. They left the muggy air of the tennis courts and entered the over-cooled casino. Tiff shivered.

The carpet looked more appropriate for a carnival than a hotel. The red, blue, and yellow swirls of color were disorienting. Tiff took in the view of the casino. The two girls were standing in the lower level of the building, away from the mirrors and loud slot machines. This floor had everything a teenager would want—a huge arcade area, a laser tag game, a swimming pool, and shopping. There was even a small movie theater.

What would it be like to be the daughter of one of the people who ran this place? It must be like heaven to hang out here anytime you wanted. Tiff wondered how Lorna felt about it, about being rich, but was too embarrassed to ask. Asking someone directly about their finances was considered rude in her culture.

"Hey," said Lorna as they got to the ice cream parlor, "we should have a girl's night at my house sometime. We could invite some girls from the team. You know, watch movies, eat chocolate, do our nails."

They both laughed but Tiff was unsure whether Lorna was serious about the nail thing. She glanced at her nails and then at Lorna's. While hers were kept clipped short, Lorna's were nicely shaped, with a French manicure. She decided that they hadn't laughed for the same reasons.

"That would be great," she quickly replied. Tiff wondered whether her parents would say yes. She wanted more than anything to be like a normal kid and do normal things. A normal white kid, she corrected herself. While other kids got to hang out with their friends, Tiff and her brother, Hanju, had to work in the family-owned cleaners. When they weren't at work, they were expected do extra homework so they could go to college and have a good future. She sighed.

"Cool, I'll ask my mom," said Lorna, suggesting that it would be the perfect way to celebrate the end of winter quarter.

That was another thing Tiff liked about Lorna. Not only was she easygoing and liked sports, but she was equally concerned about grades. Tiff just had to convince her mom to let her stay at Lorna's. Maybe if she played up the whole "celebrating grades" angle. She had done really well this quarter. Not that bad grades were ever acceptable in her universe.

Tiff squinted through the glass case in the brightly lit room. She looked at all the fun kinds of ice cream. What hadn't she tried yet? She loved to try new things. Lorna ordered mocha almond fudge.

"Raspberry Blast, please," Tiff ordered. She wasn't even sure she liked raspberries. She followed Lorna to a tall, round table with high, red seats.

As they licked their cones, Tiff studied Lorna. She was perfect, like some kind of angel, with strawberry blonde hair; a long, straight nose; and a tall, thin build. She was everything Tiff was not. Just being with her made Tiff feel proud, and, if she was honest, a little jealous.

"So, tell me about your life," said Lorna, as if this were the most natural conversation starter in the world.

"My life?"

"Yeah, you know, your family, your past, and your dreams for the future, all that good stuff."

"Uh, that's a lot of stuff for the ten minutes we have."

Lorna seemed unfazed. She wrinkled her nose and Tiff noticed a light smattering of freckles across it.

"True. Okay, tell me one thing about you that nobody else knows."

"Wow, you really ask hard questions," laughed Tiff. Lorna just stared at her, waiting for a reply. Tiff's mind raced through the possibilities. There weren't many secrets to share. She didn't know Lorna well enough to share too many things. Not that she had a lot of juicy secrets. She did have one thing that nobody knew, but it might freak Lorna out to learn about her part in rescuing a girl from a sex slavery ring. No, that would not be a good thing to share at the beginning of their friendship.

Thoughts flitted through her mind as she looked for an innocuous thing to share. "Well, nobody but my family knows that I was born left-handed and my mom made me switch to right, so now I'm ambidextrous."

Lorna broke out in a huge grin. "So *that's* why you can hit so hard both ways! You're gonna be my secret weapon when we play doubles!"

Tiff leaned back in her chair and smiled.

CHAPTER THREE
SAMMY

Tiff lay on her stomach wearing flannel pajamas, talking with her best friend, Sammy. Her fingers pulled at the fringed bedspread as they spoke.

Sammy, whom she'd met in summer school, attended a different high school. They only managed to see each other once a month, but they stayed close through phone calls and Facebook. Texting was out because Sammy didn't have a cell phone.

"So, how's Lando?" asked Tiff, who knew it was a required question for a friend to ask.

"He's good," Sammy said softly, in an uncharacteristically dreamy way. Sammy had changed considerably since they'd first met. Tiff remembered her first impression of Sammy sitting in their small group in Mr. Monahan's English class. She was tiny, wearing all black, with long black hair and thick makeup. The whole get-up shouted "stay away from me." Sammy was softer now. She seemed healed in some deep way after all they'd been through last summer. And now she and Lando were a couple and Sammy was downright gushy. Tiff shook her head.

"You sound happy, Sammy."

"I am, but I miss you. When can we get together?"

"Probably not 'til the first-Saturday lunch, but that's only a week away."

Tiff and her three friends from last summer's class met on the first Saturday of each month at Denny's. Sometimes it was hard even to have that much time together since they all went to different high schools and were involved in different things. Lando was on the debate team and Ty had science stuff. Her stomach squeezed a bit, thinking of Ty. Oh, how she missed him…

Sammy interrupted as if she'd read Tiff's thoughts. "So … any news from Ty?"

"No. How could I get news?"

Ty and Tiff had almost been together last summer. But her strict family had forbidden her to date a black guy. Well, they had said fifteen was too young to date, period. But she knew it didn't help that he wasn't Korean, and it really didn't help that he was African American.

She still felt awful about the whole thing. Like she wanted to crawl in a hole and never come out, because she knew Ty had been super hurt by it. Why wouldn't he be? She would have been, if his family had treated her that way. But his family had been nothing but nice to her.

Sammy's voice brightened. "Well, Lando said Ty and that girl from his chemistry class broke up. Lando thinks he was just going out with her to make you jealous, anyway, and when it didn't work, he just gave her up."

"It did work! Is he blind? I was crazy jealous, but what could I do about it?" She flopped face-down on the pillow in frustration.

"Yeah, sorry about that."

Tiff propped herself up her side. "Oh, Sammy, I wish we could trade lives for a while. Your mom doesn't care that Lando is from El Salvador."

"That's true, Tiff, but I'm pretty sure you wouldn't want to change lives with me. For one thing, you'd have to put up with Itty-Bitty-Charity."

Tiff could hear Sammy's little sister shriek in the background, so she knew Sammy must have tickled her. She could picture the gap-toothed seven-year-old on the floor next to Sammy's bed, where she liked to color.

"Are you kidding me? I'd trade Charity for Hanju any day." Hanju was Tiff's younger, yet taller, brother. In truth, they'd been getting along better since last summer, but she still felt her parents favored him.

"What's the 'little emperor' done now?"

"Well, last night he asked the 'rents if he could go with his school on a ski trip because he was on the honor roll, and they said yes! Can you believe that? They would never let me go."

"That's so unfair."

"I know!" Tiff sat up and leaned against her headboard. She stared at the poster of Serena Williams smashing a ball directly across from her. "I want to ask my mom if I can spend the night at this girl's house next weekend. But I'm, like, totally scared to do it. Then he just waltzes in and asks for a ski trip and gets it."

"Whose house?"

"I told you about Lorna, the new girl from tennis? She wants to have a sleepover with girls from the team. She's super rich and it would be lots of fun."

"You should just ask, 'cause it's not fair for them to say yes to Hanju and no to you."

"I know." Sometimes Tiff didn't think even Sammy could understand about her parents. Things were just different in her family, even though Sammy's family had been through hard times and Tiff would never wish for that. She loved her parents and the grands who lived with them, but it would be so different to "just ask," like Sammy could, and expect a yes. Nothing was that simple in her family.

"I'm just scared they'll say no—but enough about my sad life. What's new with you?"

"Well, Lando got the homecoming pics back and sent one to me in the mail. It looks so funny with me all awkward in that dress—you know I hate dresses! And there's Lando with his huge grin ..."

"Oh, I can't wait to see it. Can either of you scan it for Facebook?" Tiff had only seen Sammy in a dress twice. Showing more of her body was hard for Sammy because of all of the abuse, and the self-cutting that followed the abuse. Her arms were lined with white scars. But during the summer she had become more confident and willing to wear short sleeves and dresses.

"Not me, unless I can figure out how to do it at school. I'll ask Lando."

"Hey, how goes the play? Have you heard from Dawna? How is she? How ..."

Sammy laughed. "Slow down! How can I answer all those at once? Dawna and I chat online sometimes. She is doing good back in Sierraville. You know, after the kidnapper's trial, the town welcomed her home like some kind of hero. So, she's glad to be back, even though she said it was kind of awkward at first. I miss her."

"I bet." Tiff had been slightly jealous of how close Dawna and Sammy became when Dawna moved to Reno. But she'd also seen how Sammy had blossomed. She needed a friend at her own school. Everyone needs a friend at school. She hoped Sammy wouldn't be hurt if she and Lorna became better friends.

Sammy interrupted her thoughts, "… and the play is coming along great and rehearsals are going well. I can't believe we only have six weeks! I'm so glad the crew had time to prepare last semester. I'm still tracking down props."

"Well, that's what stage managers do," said Tiff with pride in her voice. She loved how Sammy's artistic work had been acknowledged and now graced the sets for McQueen High's spring musical, *Man of LaMancha*. It was Dawna's sewing ability that landed both of them on the stage crew for costumes, and eventually Sammy was asked to be the stage manager. All of this would have been impossible for Tiff to imagine when they met last summer. There was a sharp rap on Tiff's bedroom door, a notice of lights out and quiet in the Cho household.

"Well, gotta go now. Talk later."

"Okay, bye," said Sammy.

Tiff thought about the difference between old and new friends. Old ones didn't need explanations. They knew you and understood you. It was comfortable. New friends had lots of questions. It was scary and kind of fun at the same time.

Tiff wondered at how much Sammy had changed in the last six months. *Have I changed?* Her commitment last summer had been to be and say whatever she wanted, without the constant editing her culture required. She wanted to be comfortable in her own skin. To be the sporty, loud, fun girl she was at heart. *I guess I've grown in that area. But I wish I was more of a risk-taker.*

She thought about her friends. Lando had taken huge risks toward his goal of becoming a lawyer by joining the debate team. Sammy was doing all this crazy drama stuff to help herself grow as an artist. Ty was busy applying for early admission to colleges because he wanted to be a scientist and find a cure for cancer.

Her heart pulled at the thought of Ty.

What am I doing to work toward my own goals? Do I even have goals? I like playing tennis, but is that enough? She had felt the most alive last summer when they were trying to figure out how to help Dawna. Sammy and Lando even credited Tiff for giving them direction for their futures. Yet she had no direction. It seemed like she was drifting back to who she was before they'd rescued Dawna. Tiff felt as if she was slipping into depression as she compared her life to those of her friends.

Enough of that, she concluded, *this semester I'm going to be a risk-taker. That is my new goal. I will find some way to be significant. Look out, world!*

Chapter Four
The Blue Group

Ty watched Tiff across the restaurant table as she savored her pancakes. Her mouth was endlessly fascinating to him. She had full, perfect lips and straight, white teeth. He shook his head. What was the matter with him? This was getting ridiculous! He was the logical, clear-headed one, yet he couldn't stop obsessing about her even when he sat right across from her at Denny's. He thought he must be crazy. Why not enjoy the present? He was actually with her, right now. *Pay attention, idiot!*

"Ty," Lando said, apparently not for the first time because he was snapping his fingers in front of Ty's nose. "I said, do you want to tell the girls about your dream?"

"Huh … oh. Uh, okay." He felt so stupid. He glanced around the room to help himself focus, taking in the busy restaurant, crowded booths, and sweet smell of maple syrup. This monthly lunch was usually the time when he felt most comfortable, yet now he felt anything but. Lando and Sammy were snuggled together at end of the booth, and that didn't help. He knew it looked like they were on a double date, which just made it worse. Yet there was no one else he could talk to about his dreams—only Sammy, Tiff, and Lando.

They were with him through it all last summer and would understand. "Well, it's not much, really. It's just that I haven't had a dream that vivid since the ones last summer about Dawna."

"Who was it about?" asked Sammy, leaning forward.

"I don't know. I was just standing outside this white house and it felt really scary." He looked up at Tiff to see her raise an eyebrow; her dimple deepened. "And," he added quickly, "when I went onto the porch, I heard a girl scream."

Sammy and Tiff gasped. "What happened next?" asked Sammy.

"That's it."

"Well," began Tiff, "that's disturbing." She stabbed a pancake with her fork.

"I'll say," added Sammy.

"Yeah," said Ty, "not much to go on, I know. Have any of you had any … odd things happen?"

He referred to special gifts they had each discovered last summer. Sammy had drawn sketches about Dawna at the same time Ty was having dreams about her. Lando just seemed to know certain things that helped when they needed information. Recently, they'd used their gifts again to help find a missing boy up in Loyalton.

Then there was Tiff. He didn't know if her ideas were a gift or just part of her personality, but she had a kind of encouraging way about her that made people feel like they could do anything.

His gaze scanned each face, looking for a sign that he wasn't alone with this dream.

"Nothing," said Tiff.

"Nada," added Lando.

"Nil," finished Sammy.

"Well, then, I guess we just wait." Ty set down his glass and the three nodded in agreement. That was one of the hardest lessons they had learned last summer. You can't rush this kind of information. It came when it came. It frustrated them all, but it was true. "So, what else is new?"

"Well, I have some news!" Tiff said with a huge smile. "My mom is actually gonna let me spend the night over at my new friend Lorna's house. She's having some girls over from the tennis team. And at first my mom said, 'No way,' but then Lorna's mom actually showed up at the cleaners with a ton of clothes. When she asked my mom if I could stay over, I think she couldn't refuse!"

"That's great," said Ty. He knew what a victory this was for Tiff. Her parents were overprotective. He tried not to show the pain he felt whenever he thought of her parents' rejection of him. They had not allowed her to go with him to his homecoming dance last semester. It was a hard blow and his rebound relationship with Sheila had just been stupid. Now he wanted Tiff back, but didn't know how to tell her.

"That's great," he said again, lamely.

"Yeah, didn't you say she was rich?" asked Sammy. A long red bang dangled into one of her eyes. The rest of her hair was cut short, which matched her pixie body.

"She is," agreed Tiff. "Her dad's a bigwig in the casino industry."

"My mom's a bigwig in the casino, too!" laughed Lando as he stabbed an uneaten pancake from Sammy's plate and put it on his own. "In cleaning them, anyway!"

They all laughed with him.

"You'll have to take notes and tell us all about what her house looks like. Give us the scoop on how the rich and famous live," said Sammy.

"I will. I can't wait to see her house, but that's not why I'm going. She's super nice, and a great tennis player, and a good student, too."

"She sounds perfect," said Lando.

"She sounds like you," said Ty. The words slipped out before he could catch them, and now he felt his face flush hot. Tiff looked directly at him but he didn't take it back.

"Thanks," she said quietly, her eyebrows knitted together.

Sammy jumped in. "I have news, too. I heard from the Loyalton group; Dawna and all of them are coming down to see the spring musical."

"That's amazing," said Tiff. "It will be so great to see them all again."

"When is the play?" asked Ty, as he pulled out his phone. "I need to put it in my calendar."

"It's the first weekend in March. I'm getting pretty excited! The girl playing Dulcenea is wonderful! She has jet black hair and will look amazing in the dresses Dawna made."

Lando cut in, "And I got to see Sammy's sets under the lights, and they look really cool." Sammy beamed at him.

"I can't wait to come!" said Tiff. "Should we all plan to be there opening night or closing night? Or maybe the one in between?"

"I'm going every night," said Lando. Sammy blushed at this. Ty smiled to himself, but he envied Lando's happiness.

Sammy said, "Dawna's group is coming opening night and I'd like you all to be there so we can go out afterwards and celebrate. Saturday night will be the cast party and I'll be busy."

"Sounds good to me," said Ty. He turned to Tiff. "I can pick you up." Then he noticed her wide eyes and added, "And Lando, too, of course."

~

THE BOYS FOLLOWED THE GIRLS OUT to the parking lot. This is usually where they parted ways. Tiff and Sammy waited for Tiff's dad. Lando and Ty went to Ty's car. Ty liked to leave before Tiff's dad arrived, but today he needed to talk to her. As the restaurant door closed behind him, he called out, "Tiff, wait up."

She slowed and Lando and Sammy moved off together, giving Ty and Tiff a bit of privacy. She turned to him with an unwavering gaze. Her face was mostly covered in a scarf and hat against the icy wind.

Ty felt his stomach tighten, but it was now or never. "Tiff, I'm sorry about everything that ..."

"No, I'm sorry," she cut in. "I'm sorry about my folks and the dance and ... everything." She hung her head.

He gently lifted her chin. "Tiff, I want to be with you. I don't care about all that. How can we make this work?"

She pulled her chin away, avoiding eye contact. "It won't work, Ty. There's no way."

"I don't believe that. There has to be a way."

She started to turn toward Sammy. He grabbed her arm. "How about this: Just for now, we could IM each other at night."

Tiff turned. She laughed, shaking her head. "Instant message? Is that enough for you?"

"Of course, Tiff, I just want some contact. I need to talk to you. I need you."

Her face flushed and she looked to the parking lot behind her. He followed her gaze and saw her dad's car pull into the far driveway. He let go of her arm and headed toward his car. "Every night at eight," he said with confidence as he slipped into his car. She didn't say no but turned toward her ride, then over her shoulder shouted, "Okay. But not tonight, I'm going to a sleepover!" Doing a happy jig, she danced away.

Ty felt like he'd just won the lottery.

CHAPTER FIVE
THE SLEEPOVER

Mrs. Cho insisted on walking Tiff to the door to greet Lorna's mother. She wrote down the family's phone number and then gave an approving nod as she scanned the interior of the marbled entrance way. To Tiff's delight, her mother didn't stay around, just made a few admiring statements about the house and left.

Tiff was the first to arrive and was glad, because Lorna offered her a tour of their home. The first thing she saw upon arriving was a huge entrance hall with a wide, curving staircase up to the second floor. The air had a fresh lemon scent to it. The staircase was stunning, with a chandelier that sent rainbows of color down into the room below. Downstairs, Lorna took Tiff into the great room, which was a large sitting room with a huge marble fireplace and brown leather couches. Tiff was impressed with the feel of the home; it was not cold and protected, as she had envisioned. She realized she thought rich people would flaunt their wealth with impractical décor like plush white carpets and glass tables. This home was full of earth tones and comfortable furniture. The wood floors were covered in rugs of rich dark tapestries. Tiff loved it.

Then Lorna showed her the media room. It was like a small theater with a huge flat-screen TV and six small, cozy, red velvet loveseats that faced the TV, each with a lap blanket tossed over it for snuggling.

"This is amazing!" said Tiff.

"Thanks," said Lorna smiling. "I thought tonight we could watch a movie if people want to. My dad has hundreds of movies, or we can stream one on the Internet."

"That sounds fun. Who all is coming?"

"Turns out, Summer had to bail and most everyone else is out of town or busy, so it's just you, me, Toni, and Kristin."

"Oh, I like Toni, and Kristin is lots of fun. It will be a great night. Can I see your room?"

"Sure." Just then the doorbell rang and Lorna dragged Tiff back through the open hallway to the front door. Lorna's mom, Mrs. Molinari, got there at the same time the girls did. She pulled open the heavy wooden door and Tiff was relieved to see Kristin and Toni standing there, with Kristin's mother. Tiff was the only non-white girl there, but she was used to that. Most of her friends at school were white. Toni was a sophomore, like Tiff, and Kristin a junior, like Lorna.

After greetings all around, the girls headed upstairs to Lorna's room. Tiff didn't know what she had expected, but was surprised to find that it wasn't much different from her own bedroom. It was bigger, of course. Lorna had a queen-sized bed while Tiff had a double. But the feel of the room was very teenagery, with posters of musicians and tennis stars, trophies on the bookcase and paperbacks scattered on the shelves. Her room had one thing Tiff's did not: a foosball table.

"Foosball?" Tiff shouted and ran to pick a side. The others joined her and soon a raucous game was in play. Tiff loved foosball. She loved to twist her wrists to slam the soccer ball down the court to make a goal. Lorna was on her side of the table and Kristin and Toni faced them. The girls whooped and hollered until Mrs. Molinari stuck her head in the room. She shook her head, laughed, and said over her shoulder as she walked away, "I have dessert when you're ready."

It didn't take long for them to be ready. As they ran down the staircase, Tiff and Lorna sang the *Rocky* theme song, fists in the air, with Kristin and Toni gently pushing them forward. "Rematch after snack," shouted Kristin.

"Yeah, rematch!" agreed Toni.

In the kitchen, Lorna led the way to seats around a high center island. There was a stove and sink on one side, and a long seating area on the other. The subtle differences in the way the rich lived began to dawn on Tiff. While her own kitchen at home smelled like her mother's and grandmother's yummy cooking, this one smelled more like cleaning fluid. Maybe Mrs. Molinari wasn't much of a cook. Maybe being rich was not as glamorous as she'd first believed, but there were subtle differences. For instance, Mrs. Molinari looked a little too perfect. She was probably the same age as Tiff's mother, but her figure and face were impossibly young. Her shoulder-length hair, a perfect blend of various shades of blonde and red highlights, was swept back on one side and held by a jeweled barrette. Her finger nails were fake but beautiful. *I wonder if Lorna looks like her mom or her dad*, thought Tiff. Lorna had reddish-blonde hair, like her mom, but who knew whether that was her mom's natural color? And although Lorna was tall and thin, Mrs. Molinari was short and curvy.

Lorna didn't look like her mother at all, but maybe plastic surgery had changed the woman's face. Tiff had seen a photo of Lorna's parents in the entryway. Her dad was handsome, with dark Italian features.

Another difference was evident when Mrs. Molinari brought out dessert. Whereas her mom might bring out ice cream and a homemade dessert, Mrs. Molinari offered a fancy cake that obviously had come from a bakery, and then two more desserts, each very fancy, and very not-homemade. There was a tower of cupcakes in different flavors and some small, pretty cups with custard and sprinkles. Tiff wondered why Mrs. Molinari had gone to all this trouble for four teenage girls. They would have been happy with store-bought cookies and milk. It felt like overkill. Plus, once she served the desserts, Mrs. Molinari left the girls alone.

Tiff was pretty sure her mother would have stayed in the room and grilled each of the girls about her family and how she was doing in school. Actually, Tiff didn't know if this was true, because she'd never had a sleepover, or been to one, for that matter. She hoped she knew how to act in this situation. But soon the girls were talking, laughing, and eating, and Tiff lost her fear about not fitting in. She felt comfortable. Lorna was the perfect hostess. She was not going to think about her mom any more tonight. Or about the talk she'd had with Ty after lunch. Nope, she was determined to push it from her mind. Tonight she was only going to relax and have fun.

CHAPTER SIX
TRUTH OR DARE

After they had watched a comedy in the home theater, the girls tromped up to Lorna's room. They tried a couple of board games, but eventually Kristin suggested they play Truth or Dare, so they sat cross-legged on the carpet to play. Tiff had never played Truth or Dare but had heard of it in reference to coed parties in which kissing was involved.

This turned out to be the milder version, and Tiff began to enjoy it. The first time she chose "dare," she had to stand in Lorna's back yard, next to a manmade pond so huge it actually had a swimming float and a rowboat on it. She had to crow like a rooster at the top of her lungs. She didn't feel too embarrassed because there were no neighbors close enough to hear her. But it was cold! She got it over with as fast as she could and they all raced back upstairs to get warm.

The next time it was her turn she chose "truth." After all, what did she have to hide? But leave it to Toni to ask a personal question.

"Do you have a boyfriend or a guy you like?"

Three sets of eyes bored into Tiff as she squirmed in her seat. How much should she share? "Well," she began, "it's complicated!"

The girls laughed at this. Encouraged, she went on. "There's this guy I really like."

"Oooh," said Kristin.

"But my folks won't let me date yet, so I don't get to see him very often." Tiff grabbed a magazine off the floor and opened it.

"Oh, no, you don't," Kristin grabbed the magazine from Tiff's hand and tossed it aside. "We want details!"

Tiff took a deep breath. She'd never talked about Ty to anyone but Sammy before. Should she trust her secret with these girls? *Well, it's not like they'll ever meet him.* "Okay. His name is Ty and he goes to Hug High and he's black." She watched their faces, to see if they would react negatively, as her parents had. Lorna's eyebrows went up and she smiled. Toni had more to say.

"Oh, I just love black guys! White guys are so boring."

"I don't think my mom would let me date a black guy," added Kristin. "Did your folks have a problem with that?"

"They only want me to date Korean guys. And, I can promise you, that is not going to happen."

"Why not?" Toni said. "I like Korean guys."

"You like all guys!" said Kristin.

"True," agreed Toni, as they all laughed.

"Tiff," interrupted Lorna, "tell us more about Ty."

Then it was like the stopper had been pulled out of the bottle; she began to gush. "Well he's tall, good-looking, and really good at science. He's amazing at the piano, and he has a really serious way about him. When he thinks hard, his head tilts to one side ..." she stopped, aware she was saying way too much.

"Oh, you have it bad, girl!" said Toni.

Tiff flushed and smiled. But the girls looked at her, expecting to hear more. "Well, I got to see him today," she blurted.

"What?" said Lorna. "Today? How did you get to see him?"

"Uh, well, once a month I get together with some friends for lunch. We met last June in summer school at McQueen. So ... that's when I get to see him."

"What did he say?" asked Kristin. "Does he want to go out with you?"

"Well, actually ... yes," smiled Tiff. "After we ate at Denny's and were walking to the parking lot, he pulled me aside. He was like, 'I know we can't go out right now, but I need you. Can we at least find some way to communicate?'"

"Wow! Did he really say, 'I need you?'" asked Toni, eyes wide. "What did you say?"

"Well, we decided to chat on Facebook every night at eight."

"Ohmygosh. That's so romantic!" said Lorna. "But it's past eight, Tiff. You missed him."

"Oh no, he knew we wouldn't talk tonight."

"Facebook!" yelled Kristin. "Let's Facebook stalk him right now!"

Lorna ran to get her laptop and the girls spent several minutes ogling Ty's profile and pictures.

Toni grabbed for the keyboard. "Let's write him a message. We'll tell him of Tiff's undying love!"

Tiff reached for the keyboard and the two started to wrestle.

Lorna stepped in. She yanked the keyboard from both girls. "Hey, knock it off, Toni, unless you want us to write notes about your undying love on a certain point guard's wall."

Toni's hands went up in a motion of surrender. "No, thanks, I'm good."

The girls laughed and began to tease Toni.

Tiff felt relieved to have the focus shift to Toni. It felt good to think of Ty and tell her friends about him. But if she let herself think about him anymore, she might not be able to stop. And she wanted to enjoy every part of her first sleepover. She could think about Ty later.

"Lorna," she said over the tease fest, "truth or dare?" The girls' attention turned back to the game.

"Um ... truth!"

Payback time, thought Tiff. "Tell us something about yourself that nobody or almost nobody knows!"

Lorna sat silent for a minute, and pulled on the carpet. Tiff began to wonder if she'd asked a bad question.

Finally, Lorna looked up. "I'm adopted."

"Really?" asked Tiff. *So that's why she doesn't look like her parents.*

"Yeah, I was a baby when they adopted me. I don't really know anything about my birth dad. The only thing they'll tell me about my birth mom is that social services took me away from her because I wasn't safe."

"Do you ever want to meet her?" asked Kristin.

"I don't think so," Lorna shook her head. "My parents are great, and they're the only parents I've ever known. Maybe when I'm older I'll change my mind. But I doubt it."

"Wow," said Toni as she gestured around the room. "You landed in a much better place, didn't you?"

Tiff thought the same thing, but wouldn't have said it out loud. She held her breath to see how Lorna would take the question.

Lorna answered with a smile. "I did, didn't I?"

CHAPTER SEVEN
CHATTING

Ty readied himself for his fist Facebook chat with Tiff. He wondered if she'd be there. What should he say? How should he begin? Finally his phone reminder buzzed and he typed the first thing that came into his mind.

"How was the party?"

There, that was innocuous. He waited, hopeful and nervous. *Would she be there?*

"It was awesome!" responded Tiff with a smiley-face emoticon.

Ty breathed a sigh of relief and settled back against his desk chair.

"Tell me about it."

"Well, the house was amazing. Gorgeous furniture, and we watched a movie in this little theater! It even had a popcorn maker right in the room!"

"Seriously?"

Ty tried to picture Tiff. Did she have a goofy grin on her face like he did?

"Yep, and Lorna has a foosball table right in her bedroom, too."

"Dang, I love foosball!"

"I know, huh. And, we played Truth or Dare!"

"What?"

For a moment he stopped breathing. Were there boys at this party?

"I thought that was a kissing game. Is there something you need to tell me?"

"Yes, actually there is … I'm a chicken!"

"Huh?"

"I took a dare and had to go out by this manmade lake and squawk like a chicken."

Ty shook his head at the innocence of it all, relieved.

"They have their own lake?"

"Yep! And it's big enough to swim in and has a diving platform and a row boat. Lorna said if we come over this summer we can swim in it."

"Amazing. I miss you!"

Ty pictured Tiff as she received this new information. What would she say? A witty quip, or something he longed to hear. When she finally replied, it was not what he'd expected.

"I told the girls about you."

He smiled. "You did?"

"Well, on a dare. But then I told them everything. We even Facebook stalked you!"

"Oh no, did they look at my pictures?"

"Yep, they especially liked the one of your kindergarten graduation."

"I seriously need to kill my sister for hacking my profile."

"Lol! Which sister?"

"Machelle."

"Aw, don't take it off, it's cute!"

"If you say so."

"It is! I love it."

"Are your parents on Facebook?"

"No, are you kidding me? Why?"

"I was wondering if I should change my status to 'in a relation-ship.'"

Ty held his breath. What would she say to this idea? Were they in a relationship? The curser pulsed. What would he do if she said no? What if she just wanted to be friends?

He prompted her. "You there?"

"Yeah, can we be in a relationship without it being Facebook-official?" she replied.

Ty was worried. Why would she want to keep their relationship a secret?

"Why don't you wanna be FBO?"

"Cause, my parents aren't on Facebook, but my brother is, and most of the kids from my church."

Ty tried not to feel bad about this; after all, it seemed she wanted to be in a relationship, just not a public one.

"Sure," he typed, trying to sound like it was no big deal. "Can we at least tell Sammy and Lando?"

"I already told Sammy, and she already told Lando!"

Ty grinned. So she was excited about this. "You stole my news!"

She sent a smiley face.

"Well, then, we're official, I guess."

"I guess we are," she replied.

He sent a smiley face.

CHAPTER EIGHT
SHEILA

What fascinated Ty most about himself these days was how a highly rational, scientific, level-headed person could suddenly become a total idiot over a girl. If it had been anybody else, he would have mocked that person mercilessly. What had happened? Suddenly he had a hard time being attentive in class and caught himself smiling for no apparent reason. His sisters noticed and began to tease him. When he missed a chemistry question, even Mr. Zimmerman looked at him like he suspected something was wrong. But nothing was wrong, everything was right. He and Tiff chatted every night, and he felt like a fool as he waited for eight o'clock to come so he could send her his hello.

Somehow it became understood that he would initiate the chat. He always sat at his desk when he chatted with her. He daydreamed about what to say and tried to find different, interesting greetings. He'd tried, "Greetings Earthling," "Howdy Partner," and "Wassssup!" The tone of his greeting led to a flurry of banter. It was a fun way to break the ice.

Then, usually, the news turned to the highlights of the day. This was Ty's favorite part. He liked to picture Tiff propped up on her bed, laptop on her lap. It felt as if they were sitting together talking in some quiet café. They limited themselves to an hour so they could finish their homework.

Then came the awkward part: how to say goodbye. He still wasn't sure how much to tell Tiff about how he felt. He didn't want to ruin what they had by being pushy, but it bugged him that they couldn't see each other face to face.

He stood, staring at his locker, as the school emptied around him. A hand touched his shoulder and he smelled jasmine.

"Did you fall asleep in there?" asked a familiar silky voice.

"Hi, Sheila." Ty turned to see his ex-girlfriend next to him, her arms full of books.

"You sure have been daydreamy lately. Something on your mind?"

There was something on his mind, but there was no way he was going to tell Sheila about it. "Just lots to think about, I guess…"

Sheila looked at him seriously. "Tyrell, can I talk to you?"

Ty was not interested in being cornered into another conversation about why he had broken up with her. "I thought that's what we were doing."

"No, I'm serious, I need someone to talk to, and I don't have anyone to talk to but you."

Ty began shoving books into his locker. He didn't want to talk to Sheila. He wanted to think about Tiff. He looked at her more closely. Of all the black girls in his school, Sheila was the most beautiful. Some of the girls straightened their hair; many had extensions. But

Sheila kept hers soft and natural. She was stunning. He remembered touching that hair; it was as soft as lamb's wool.

He shook his head to clear the thought. Sheila looked upset. Even the regal bearing and ebony skin of her Ethiopian mother could not hide the dark circles under her perfect makeup. "Okay," he said reluctantly, "I've got time now. You want to go find an empty classroom or something?"

"Could we talk in your car?"

Ty did not want to talk to Sheila in his car. Everyone in the school would see it and then the rumor mill, which had just begun to die down, would kick up again. Besides, he had kissed her in that car. "I'd rather not sit in the car; it's too cold," he said lamely.

"Tyrell, it's important. I don't know who else to talk to. It's private." She stared at him, her red lips pouting, and she gave him puppy dog eyes until his will begin to soften.

"Okay, but we're not going to sit in the parking lot. We'll just drive around."

"I don't know what you're so afraid of. You act like I'm going to bite you or something. It's not like I haven't been in your car before."

Is she baiting me? "I'm not afraid of anything." He slammed his locker a little too hard and headed to the parking lot a little too fast so she had to trot in her ridiculous high-heeled snow boots to keep up. He thought about Tiff and the practical, sporty way she dressed. It made so much more sense than Sheila's heels, which made her almost his height and looked impossible to walk in. What had he ever seen in her, anyway?

At his Subaru, he unlocked her door but didn't open it. He knew he was being a jerk but didn't care. With exaggerated motions, he jerked open his car door and fastened his seatbelt. Sheila got in slowly, frowning.

Ty wanted to head off any discussion of their relationship. He drove to the exit lane, which now only had a few cars in it because of his dawdling. Ty mentally kicked himself. *If I'd left right away I would have missed her.*

Glancing in the rearview mirror, he noticed a car full of girls pointing at his car and laughing. *Great, now it will be all over school.*

He pulled onto the street, faster than necessary, and into the turning lane toward her house.

"Sheila, I don't want to rehash why we broke up. That discussion is over. I've … moved on."

She turned to look at him; her face showed lines of strain. "I was afraid of that. Is it someone from our school? I'd like to know so I can be ready to see you with someone else."

"No, it's nobody you know."

"That Tiffany girl you told me about from last summer?"

Ty was silent.

"I knew it, I knew it was her! Tyrell, I can't believe you'd date someone whose parents won't let her be with you because you're black!"

"Hey, it's not Tiff's fault."

"I knew you weren't over that girl." Sheila shook her head. "I just knew it."

They sat in silence at a stoplight. The ever-present Reno sun glared through the windshield, even though it was cold enough to see their breath inside the car.

Sheila broke the silence. "Is she why you broke up with me?"

Ty shot her a warning look. "I already said we were not going to talk about this. Now, tell me what you wanted to say so I can drive you home."

Sheila turned up the pout. She silently pulled her coat more tightly around her. Finally, she sighed. "I got a letter from my mother."

"Your mother?"

Now he understood why Sheila wanted to talk to him. None of her other friends knew about her mother. Her father had met her mother on a cultural exchange in Ethiopia during college. Eight months after his return to the States, he received a letter explaining that he was the father of a baby girl. He went back to Africa to see if he could work out some arrangement with Sheila's mother, but it didn't take long for him to realize that the ebony beauty was insane. She wanted nothing to do with her own child and insisted he take Sheila back with him to America at once. Embarrassed about her history, Sheila told her friends that her mother was dead, and the lie had stuck.

"Wait, you told me she didn't even speak English. How did she write you?"

"She must have gotten someone to write it for her."

"What did she say?"

"She wants me to come back."

"To Ethiopia?"

"Yes, to live with her."

"You can't do that. You don't even know her. You're not African, you're American. You don't even speak her language!"

"I know all that."

"Then what's the problem?"

"I don't know. The letter was kind of creepy."

"In what way?"

"It was like, I don't have a choice. It said, 'You will come back to me right away.'"

"Maybe it was just a mistranslation. Maybe whoever wrote it for her doesn't speak English that well either ..."

"That's what my dad said. It just kind of freaked me out. The tone was almost threatening."

"Well, it's not like she can hurt you from Ethiopia."

"That's the weird part. It had a Chicago postmark on it."

"What?"

"I know."

"Is your dad worried?"

"No, you know him, he just blows it off."

"Well, he is the chief of police. If he says not to worry, then we shouldn't worry."

Sheila looked at him and smiled, the first genuine smile Ty had seen that day. "Thanks for saying 'we,' Tyrell. You know I haven't told anyone about my mother. Having a crazy mother is not something you want to spread around. I could really use a friend right now."

"You got it, Sheila. No worries."

CHAPTER NINE
VOICES

Ever since the night of the sleepover, Lorna and Tiff had been inseparable. They played tennis together after school, if the weather was warm enough. On weekends, they played tennis on the Grand Sierra's indoor courts. Two weeks after the party at Lorna's, Mrs. Cho actually said that Lorna could spend the night at Tiff's house. Tiff waited all week for Friday night to roll around, but finally it was here and Lorna had arrived.

Tiff was worried that her house would be a disappointment. But Lorna seemed to love everything about it, even the Korean food and Tiff's grandmother, who didn't speak much English. Lorna was one of those people who just seemed to enjoy life.

They played on the Wii for a few hours in the family room until they were exhausted. Then they went to Tiff's room and flopped down on the bed.

The only topic about which the girls did not agree was music. Tiff loved popular music you could dance to, and Lorna, who had grown up in the south, liked country. It had become a challenge; Lorna tried to get Tiff to like any country song. She introduced her to a new country artist every time they got together. Tonight it was Carrie Underwood.

"She doesn't count," said Tiff. "She's a crossover artist; everybody likes her!"

"No she's not, she's country. She's won a million country music awards."

"Nope, she doesn't count."

"Hey, Tiff," Lorna turned serious, "can I tell you a secret?"

"You mean that you're in love with that Travis Tritt guy? Yeah, I already know."

Lorna sat up on the bed and hugged her legs. "No, it's something else. It's kind of embarrassing. But you won't tell anyone, right?"

"Of course not, what is it?

"Well, I know it sounds stupid, and I hope you don't think I'm crazy, but ... I think I'm hearing voices."

"Voices, like in your head? Or with your ears?"

"No, in my head, I think."

Tiff sat up cross-legged and faced Lorna. She did not want her new friend to be crazy. But didn't crazy people hear voices? Lorna was one of the kindest, smartest, sanest people she'd ever met. It had to be something else. "Tell me more."

"Well, it started about a week ago. I was at Walmart, trying to find tennis balls, and I heard this female voice, as clear as a bell, say, 'I'm coming.'"

"'I'm coming?' That could have been anyone in the store."

"I know! I looked all around, even in the next aisle, but nobody was there."

"Maybe it was just someone over the loudspeaker."

"I thought of that, but just listen. A few days later I was in my room. I heard the same woman's voice again. It said, 'You're mine, and I'm coming to take you home.'"

"Could it have been your mom?"

"Trust me; I searched the whole house, even though I knew my mom wasn't home. Nobody was. It really freaked me out."

"I'm kind of freaking out myself right now," Tiff said. "Is this some kind of ghost story they tell at sleepovers?"

"No, Tiff, I'm serious. I'm starting to wonder if I'm crazy."

"Lorna, you're the most normal person I know."

"Well, I Googled schizophrenia and it said that it can start in adolescence. Tiff, what if I'm schizophrenic?" Lorna's voice got high and she blinked rapidly.

Tiff grabbed Lorna's arm and squeezed. "You are not crazy. Do you hear me? There has to be some other explanation."

"Like what?"

"Well, maybe you've got super-sensitive hearing suddenly and you're, like, picking up radio signals or something. You didn't get any new fillings recently, did you?"

"No, and no metal plates in my head." Lorna smiled.

"Hey, I know. Did you see the movie *Phenomenon*?"

"No, why?"

"My mom made me watch it. She's a John Travolta fan. Anyway, this guy has all these extra-special powers and, in the end, it turns out to be from a brain tumor."

Lorna just stared at Tiff.

"Yeah, sorry. That was a bad example. Sorry."

"I don't know what would be worse, to find out I had a brain tumor or that I'm schizophrenic!"

"Lorna, you're neither! Whatever it is, it only happened twice. It was just some fluke thing. You're fine."

Lorna looked only slightly relieved. "Okay, if you say so, I won't worry about it."

CHAPTER TEN
FIRST FIGHT

Tiff loved her nightly chats with Ty. She had skipped her Friday night chat when Lorna had been over, and now she was anxious to hear from him. She was ready, propped up on her bed, when his name popped up on her screen. Tonight's greeting was extra special. His "Hey, Beautiful," made her heart jump when she saw it on the screen.

She had told him all about her time with Lorna, except the part about the voices. This was a new problem—having a boyfriend you were supposed to share things with, as well as a friend who wanted you to keep a secret. She wrestled with it for a while before deciding to keep Lorna's secret. Tiff and Ty happily chatted until the mood suddenly shifted.

"Hey, Tiff, there's something I need to tell you."

Tiff braced herself. Was Ty the kind of guy to break up with her online? She didn't think so.

"What is it?"

"I talked to Sheila at school yesterday."

Tiff felt her stomach tighten. His old girlfriend? Why would Ty tell her this if it had only been a casual "hello" in the hallway?

"Uh ... okay."

"I just wanted you to know. There's nothing going on or anything, she just needed to talk because she's having some family issues."

"And she had to talk to you?"

"Yeah, it's kinda complicated. But it doesn't mean anything at all. I just thought you should know."

"Okay. Thanks ... I guess."

"You're not mad, are you? It didn't mean anything." His messages had a pleading quality. And why did he keep saying that?

"I just don't know why she had to talk to you. She has like a million friends, right?"

"Well, yeah, but none of her friends know about this specific issue."

"And you do?"

"Yes."

Tiff thought about this. There was something Ty didn't want to tell her, which should be fine. She had not told him about Lorna's voices. But somehow it felt different for her to keep the secrets of her friend than for him to share secrets with his ex-girlfriend. She felt irritated, but didn't know why.

"Tiff, are you there?"

"I'm here. But I should probably go do my homework now."

It was a full ten minutes before they usually signed off, but she felt sad for some reason. She typed, "I'll talk to you tomorrow," and closed her computer. Tears filled her eyes.

∾

TIFF SHOULDN'T HAVE BEEN surprised when Ty showed up after school on Monday. He had left a message on her phone and texted her, too. This freaked her out because her parents occasionally checked her phone, as they had after he'd invited her to the homecoming dance. She'd Facebooked him that she couldn't talk last night because of a family outing, but it hadn't been true.

She felt so confused about him talking to Sheila. All her insecurities jumped to the surface and made her feel miserable and stupid, but she didn't know what to do about it. Now here he was: He stood by his car, in the cold, and waited for her to notice him. She waved goodbye to Lorna, who gave her a wide grin before Tiff walked over to see him.

"Hey," he said as she approached.

"Hey."

"Tiff, I'm so sorry, I didn't mean to upset you. It was nothing, really."

"I know. I'm sorry." She felt stupid for being mad at him. "I don't know why it bothered me so much."

Ty reached up and pushed back a strand of Tiff's hair that had escaped her ponytail. "I don't want you to be mad at me."

She blushed and looked down. He lifted her chin up and gazed into her eyes. "And I really wanted to see you. Can we, maybe, go for a walk?"

"Okay." She signaled to Lorna and turned toward the back of the school. Ty reached out and took her hand. Tiff realized this was the first time Ty had ever held her hand. Most of their relationship had been long distance. She felt very aware of his hand—bigger, warmer, and even softer than hers. She was sure anyone who saw them would wonder who he was. She was glad Hanju was at basketball practice.

When they got near the back of the school, Ty stopped and pulled Tiff into a hug. This was her first hug with someone she was not related to. It felt odd, warm, awkward … and wonderful.

He pulled back. "Now do you believe me … that my talk with Sheila meant nothing to me?"

She nodded, unable to speak. He'd actually come to her school! Her heart beat rapidly at the risk she was taking in being with him here. But hadn't she decided this was her semester to take risks?

"Tiff, I want to see you in person. Your mom has allowed you to stay after school every day to play tennis. Do you think sometimes I could come here and we could hang out a little bit?"

She considered this. Talk about risky. Word could get back to her mom. But being with Ty in person felt so amazing, it was worth the risk.

"Okay," she answered.

"Maybe I could come one day a week?"

It felt scary to her to even think these things, let alone plan them. But he pulled her into another hug and all of her rational objections were somehow lost in his arms.

"Okay," she said into his chest.

"Okay, then, on Mondays I'll drop by, just for a little while. Okay?"

She stepped back from him. "That would be a long drive for a short visit. Ty, I wouldn't be able to see you for more than fifteen minutes."

"I know, but I would drive that far just to see you for two seconds."

Tiff looked at the ground, stunned but undecided. Ty pulled her into a hug again and kissed the top of her head. "We'll be careful, I promise. Okay?"

"Okay," she squeaked as he squeezed even harder.

He took her hand and led her back around the school to the tennis courts where Lorna hit balls against a backboard. In the crazy way of Reno weather, this week had warmed into the fifties, and it felt good to be outside. Tiff gestured for Lorna to come over.

"Lorna, this is Ty. Ty, Lorna." They shook hands and Lorna smiled.

"I feel like I already know you," said Lorna.

"I feel the same way," said Ty. "Well, I'll let you get back to your game. Tiff, could you walk with me to my car?"

As they walked, Ty said, "I need you to know that I might talk to Sheila some more in the future."

Tiff stopped in her tracks. "Why?" It came out a whine. Why was she acting this way? It was so unlike her.

"I know it's hard to understand, but Sheila has been contacted by her birth mother. She's never known her and no one but me knows she exists. She's afraid of her, so she may need a friend to talk to. That's all it is, just friendship."

Tiff thought about this. If Lorna had been contacted by her birth mother, she would need a friend to talk to for sure. Still, Sheila was Ty's ex-girlfriend. Then again, he had come all the way over here to make sure Tiff was okay. And he wanted to see her every week. She guessed he wouldn't be doing that if he was interested in Sheila, who was right there at his own school.

She nodded up at him. He pulled her into one last hug and placed a kiss on the top of her head again. Then he pulled open his car door and was gone. She watched as his car left the parking lot. What a day for firsts. Her first hand-holding, her first hugs, and her first kisses. Well, sort of, anyway. She hoped there would be more.

CHAPTER ELEVEN
CANDLES

As Ty lifted his phone, his hand shook. It was three a.m. It had happened again … another dream. He was freaked out. Why did these dreams always wake him up at three a.m.? He had hoped the first dream had been a fluke, but after this one, he could no longer dismiss them. He had to talk to someone about it. He couldn't risk a call to Tiff. He decided to call Lando. Lando was extremely rational and good at asking questions. Plus, his gift was knowing things that there were no logical means for him to know. Maybe he'd know what to do in this situation.

Ty and Lando had a signal for when they needed to talk. Lando didn't have a cell phone, but had a prepaid phone for emergencies. Ty would call and hang up before the voicemail clicked on. Then Lando would call back on his house phone. That way they didn't wake up his mom and grandma.

"What's up?" said Lando, his voice husky with sleep.

"I had another dream."

Ty heard rustling and guessed it was Lando as he sat up in bed. "What happened?" he asked, his voice less froggy.

"It was the same as last time. I walked up to a white house, and as soon as I got to the door there was this horrible scream. But this time, I started to go into the house and the door was unlocked. The house was dark, like pitch black, and at first I couldn't see anything, but it had a weird smell, like spicy or something. I took a step in and I saw this room to my right and there were candles … lots and lots of candles burning. "

"Was anyone in there?"

"Someone knelt in front of the candles, maybe it was a fireplace. I don't know. But her back was to me. At least, I think it was a her, it was too dark to tell, but my impression was that it was a woman."

"What was she doing? Was she the one that screamed?"

"I don't know, I don't think so. But as she turned to look at me, I woke up."

"Dang."

"Yeah, it really freaked me out."

"Do you remember anything else?"

Ty let his mind walk through the dream again. "She may have been holding something. Yeah, she had her hands up high in the air and something glinted in the candlelight."

"How did she have her hands up? Like was she stretching or something?"

"No, it was like she had them together, like she was holding something in them."

"Like a knife or something?"

"Yeah, like a knife or something." Ty realized what he'd just said and felt his eye begin to twitch.

"Hey, Ty, this dream is getting pretty sick."

"You don't have to tell me! That's why I called. It freaked me out."

"Okay, think. Is there anything else you remember?"

"Well, I wanted to go left, like I felt pulled to the left."

"Didn't you say you felt a pull to your left in the last dream?"

"That's right! It was the window. I think it was a bathroom window because it was small and high. When I was standing outside, my eyes kept getting pulled to that window, and when I went inside, I definitely wanted to go in that direction."

"But instead you went right?"

"Yeah. That's where freaky knife lady was."

"Was there anything in front of her, that she was going to, uh, cut with the knife?"

If there was, Ty didn't want to know. But he forced himself to think back. He couldn't see anything. Just the hands held high, the glinting of the knife thing, and her head starting to turn toward him.

"Not that I remember," he said.

"Well, that's good, anyway."

"Yeah, I guess."

"You want to call an emergency meeting with the girls?"

Ty thought about it. They would meet in a week anyway, it probably wasn't urgent.

"No, we can wait 'til our regular meeting, I guess."

"You okay to go back to sleep, then?"

"Well, do you have any of your special 'knowings' about what I should do or anything?"

"Sorry, man, I got nothing."

"Okay, yeah, I'm okay. Thanks, Lando."

"No prob. 'Night, man."

Ty lay back in his bed. He always felt better after he talked to Lando. Now maybe he could go back to sleep. But when he closed his eyes, he saw the figure of the lady with her hands raised in the candlelight. He tossed and turned. He had to think of something else.

He could think of Tiff, but that just made him frustrated. Even though he got to see her every week for fifteen minutes, it wasn't enough. He wanted more.

CHAPTER TWELVE
REVELATIONS

Tiff could tell something was wrong with Lorna the minute she walked into the fluorescent-lit lunchroom. Her normally smiling face looked tight and tense. Tiff didn't say anything about it until they'd gotten their burritos and sat down at the end of the lunch table, where most of the girls' tennis team sat. Tiff leaned across the table so no one else could hear and whispered, "Are you okay?"

Lorna gave her head a quick shake. She glanced at the other girls, who seemed involved in a discussion of their own.

"I heard it again."

"The voice?"

Lorna nodded. "During last period."

"Here, at school?" This came out louder than Tiff had meant it to.

"Shhh, Tiff, I seriously thought there was someone right behind me. I nearly jumped out of my seat. I looked behind me and there was only Billy Thompson picking his nose, as usual."

"Ewe! What did it say ... the voice?"

Lorna glanced to the left before she answered. "She said, 'You're my daughter and I'm coming for you.'"

"My daughter?"

"Tiff, what if my birth mom has found some way to contact me? Maybe we have some weird E.S.P. link and she's using it to talk to me? What if she's coming to get me?"

Tiff thought this through. It actually made more sense than the schizophrenia or the brain tumor idea, but when she saw the look on Lorna's face, she didn't want to say that out loud.

"Well, you never knew her. I doubt she could be that linked to you. Besides, you're from Florida, right? How could she even find you?"

"Oh, she could find me all right; my dad is not exactly hard to track down."

"Well, what do you really know about her, anyway?"

Lorna closed her eyes in thought. "Nothing, really. Just that the social worker said she was unsafe."

"Well, that's not encouraging. Maybe you could try to get more information from your folks."

Lorna rubbed her forehead. "Yeah, that's actually a good idea. But I think I'll try to do it without telling them about the voices."

Tiff nodded. "Good call."

"I'll let you know if I find out anything. Thanks!"

~

TIFF'S PHONE RANG AT SEVEN o'clock while she did math problems at her desk. Lorna sounded excited.

"You won't believe it, Tiff, my mom gave me this whole file they had on the adoption. She said she knew the day would come when I'd want to know more, and she just handed it to me!"

"That's amazing! What did you find out?"

"Well, her name is Debra Jean Miller. It was supposed to be an open adoption where the adoptive parents send pictures and a letter once a year, but they said the letters have been piling up at the agency for the last fifteen years! I guess Debra Jean Miller lost interest in me."

"That's great news!"

"Yeah, I guess."

Tiff heard confusion in Lorna's voice. She guessed it would be hard to know that the person who gave birth to you wasn't interested in you anymore.

"I'm sorry, Lorna. Hey, maybe something happened to her, like she died or something, and that's why she never picked them up." *Dang it!* She'd probably said the wrong thing again. She wasn't so good at this friendship thing. "I'm sorry, Lorna. That was not a good thing to say either."

"No problem. You could be right."

"Does the file say anything else about her?"

"Well, just that … where is it?" Lorna's voice trailed off. "Here, it says, 'It was determined that the parent was unfit and the home environment was unsafe.'"

"Yikes."

"Yeah, there's a caseworker's name on the file, Sandra Jones. I wonder if she could tell me any more."

"Sounds like you want to investigate."

"Yep, I'm on it, gonna do some Internet stalking first. I'll let you know if I find anything."

Tiff wasn't sure Debra Jean was somebody a person would want to find.

CHAPTER THIRTEEN
BUSTED

Tiff's heart skipped when she saw Ty's Subaru pull into Reno High's parking lot. She wrestled down the feelings of shame that came with all this deception. First, there was the fact that she met Ty at all when she knew her parents wouldn't like it. Then there was the lie that she told—that she and Lorna stayed after school on those days for tennis practice, even on days when it was snowing. The closest thing to practice they could come up with was occasionally lifting weights with the football team.

She smiled a thank you to Lorna, who waited with her under the eaves of the brick building, and then hung around until Ty left so she could give Tiff a ride home.

As Ty parked his car, Tiff walked carefully across the icy lot to meet him. He jumped out of the open door and wrapped her in a big hug. "Hi, Babe."

The sound of his mellow voice made Tiff feel warm down to her toes. She wanted to stay in his arms forever but remembered the gossip mill and how easily word could get back to her parents. She pulled away before she wanted to, and Ty tried to pull her back in, but she pushed him away. Annoyance flashed briefly across his face, and then he smiled. This was an area of tension between them. Although Ty would rather enjoy their budding romance in the open, she knew he tried to be patient with her need for secrecy. He stepped back a foot, but kept hold of her hands.

"How goes tennis practice?" he teased.

She smiled, glad the moment of discomfort had passed. "Great, now that you're here, Coach!"

He smiled broadly and she marveled at the beauty and symmetry of his teeth. He got a new look in his eye, a sparkle of something; was it yearning? Tiff knew then that he was about to kiss her, right there, in the parking lot in front of God and everyone. It was as if the world slowed down and she could see every second in sharp detail. Ty slowly bent his head toward her as a white Suburban pulled in the parking entrance next to them. Ty inched closer as the Suburban pulled up next to them.

Tiff recognized the car and stepped sideways. As the window came down, she took her hands out of Ty's grasp and he rocked back in shock, his perfect lips turned down. "Hi, Mrs. Lee," Tiff said in an overly loud voice.

The furrowed brow of the Korean lady's forehead turned from Tiff to Ty and back again, one eyebrow lifted. "Hello, Tiffany, I'm here to pick up Matthew from band practice. What are you still doing here?"

"We … had a team meeting after school. This is … John, one of our coaches."

Ty sent Tiff a death dagger, then turned to Mrs. Lee with his most charming smile. "Nice to meet you, Mrs. Lee."

Mrs. Lee was unmoved. At that moment, Lorna bounced up to

Ty's side and slipped her arm through his. "There you are, Coach! I've been looking for you." She gave Tiff a little wave and dragged Ty toward the gym.

"Let me give you a ride home, Tiffany," said Mrs. Lee. It sounded more like a command than an invitation.

"Oh, thank you, Mrs. Lee, but I have a ride home with Lorna," she gestured toward the retreating form.

"I'm sure she won't mind. Your mother would be glad to see you home safe and sound in this weather."

Tiff knew Mrs. Lee would not take no for an answer. In the Korean community, all the parents took responsibility for each other's children. The children, in turn, were expected to obey their elders.

"Thank you," Tiff said as she obediently opened the back door. The Suburban crept toward the gym. Tiff wiped the fogged window with her glove. She saw Lorna and Ty trudging toward the gym. Ty looked at his feet. *Look up!* Tiff silently pleaded. Pain clenched her chest and it was suddenly hard to breathe. She blinked back tears. She couldn't let Mrs. Lee see her cry.

∿

TIFF WAITED FOR THE OTHER shoe to drop at home. She dared not text Ty or write him online, although she was desperate to explain. She waited in terrified silence for the yelling to start. What would her mom do to her? Had Lorna's intervention been enough to fool Mrs. Lee? She sprawled on her bed and read the same paragraph from her English book over and over.

Nothing had happened by the time she was called to the dinner table. She was surprised to see an extra place setting, and when her father came out of his study, he had a young man with him, a very good-looking young man.

"Min Gee, this is Darren Kim."

Tiff blushed as Darren smiled a dimpled smile at her.

"Nice to meet you, Min Gee."

"Nice to meet you, too, but I go by Tiffany."

"Well, then, nice to meet you, Tiffany."

"And my friends call me Tiff," she added, and then regretted saying it. She sounded like a seventh-grader. *Knock it off, Tiff! You see one cute guy and get all wonky. What about Ty?*

"Well, I hope we'll be friends." He looked deeply into her eyes and she wondered if she was being hypnotized. She felt slightly woozy.

Her mother and grandmother had pulled out all the stops on this meal. How had they done it so quickly? Maybe Darren had been invited a long time ago and Tiff just hadn't paid attention. The spicy smells of rice, vegetables, and kimchee filled the air.

During dinner she learned the origin of the mystery man. A college intern, he was going to start a middle- and high-school ministry at her church. She thrilled at the idea of getting out of the Korean church service every week. Hanju's face, too, lit up at the news, and when she felt her phone buzz on her lap, she glanced down to see a text from Hanju that read, "YES!"

She sent a smiley face back. She and Hanju had developed this clandestine form of communication for the dinner table to help each other get out of troublesome situations with their folks. So far, they hadn't been caught.

She was excited about the church conversation for another reason, too. Maybe, just maybe, she hadn't been caught. Perhaps she'd dodged a bullet tonight and now had something new to look forward to on Sundays. Could it be possible? She felt her body begin to relax and she reached for more kimchee.

As the family relaxed together over dessert, and Darren complimented the meal several times, he turned his attention to Tiff and Hanju.

"I came to ask if you two will to help me with the youth ministry."

"What?" said Tiff. She did want to get out of the church service, but she didn't have any time to help start a youth ministry. She could barely keep up with school and sports as it was, plus occasionally see her secret boyfriend. She felt the phone on her lap vibrate and ignored it. A thought was beginning to form in her mind. She had not dodged a bullet. She had walked right into one. Her parents had just switched their tactics. Their new plan was to keep her too busy to see Ty. She glanced at her mother, who smiled innocently up at the handsome young man.

"Of course, my children would be more than happy to help you. It will mean they cut back on some of their other activities, but they will gladly do so for the church." Her mother turned her sweet smile toward her children, but her eyes were like steel. Tiff read in them that this was non-negotiable.

Tiff and Hanju looked at each other in panic. It was too late. It had been decided.

CHAPTER FOURTEEN
FRUSTRATION

Ty slammed his locker in frustration. Tiff would not answer her phone and wasn't even online at night for their chat. He vacillated between worry for her and anger that he had to be her secret boyfriend in the first place.

"Trouble in paradise?" a silky voice next to him said as the scent of jasmine filled the air.

Ty's back stiffened; he didn't want to deal with Sheila right now. He took a breath and reminded himself that he had promised to help her. He turned to face her.

"Hi, Sheila."

"Why so down? That pretty little Chinese girl giving you trouble?"

"She's Korean, and no, we're fine." The last word came out clipped and he knew he was giving himself away. "How are you?"

"Oh, Tyrell, you know you can't get away with lying to me. But whatever, I really need to talk to you. I got another letter and ... I'm kinda freaked."

Ty pushed down the guilty feelings growing within him. If Tiff didn't want to be seen with him, then he wasn't going to feel guilty that Sheila did. It didn't matter that Sheila was beautiful, or that they had been a couple, or that people would talk. *Let them talk!* He was sick of all the hiding.

"Want a ride home?" he asked.

"That would be great," she purred and placed a hand on his arm as they walked.

Ty knew he should shake it off, but he didn't.

"So, you got a letter?" he said with a hint of irritation when they got to his car.

Sheila reached into her handbag and pulled out the letter. She opened it to reveal the contents as he unlocked her door and held it open. She leaned over to show him the letter. It had a single line in a blocky script: "I'm coming for you."

He glanced at her in concern. "I can see why that would freak you out."

"That's not all," she said and flipped it over. "It's from Wyoming. She's closer!"

"What did your dad say?"

"I haven't shown it to him yet. But look, Tyrell, there's one more thing." She reached into the envelope and pulled out a little string of what appeared to be twisted hair. As she held it out for Ty to see, her eyes rolled back in her head and she slumped toward him.

Ty grabbed her before she could hit the ground, and she collapsed onto him. Was this a ploy to get him to hold her?

He shook her. "Sheila! Sheila!" But she was unresponsive. He maneuvered her upright onto the passenger seat and shut the door. He raced to the driver's side. Once inside, he turned to her. She looked at him now, but there was something weird about her narrowed eyes. A shiver went down his back.

"Sheila?" he said weakly. She continued to stare at him with malevolent defiance. He felt totally creeped out; this was not the Sheila he knew. What was wrong with her? He fought the urge to open the door and run. She blinked rapidly, and then shook her head. Her eyes looked more normal, but she seemed confused.

"I don't feel so good. Can you take me home?"

He turned the key in the ignition to start the engine; he couldn't get her home fast enough.

She slumped against the door and he was afraid she'd passed out again. He reached for his phone. His fingers hit his dad's number on speed dial. He knew his father was a busy pastor, but he would pick up when his son's number came up.

"Hi, son," his dad's mellow, reassuring voice answered.

"Dad, something's wrong with Sheila. Can you meet me at her house and track down her father?"

"Consider it done," he said without so much as a question.

Ty was glad his dad hadn't asked for more information. He didn't have any to give.

When he got to Sheila's house, his father was already parked outside, which meant he'd been home when Ty had called. The Duprees only lived two blocks from Sheila's family and their dads were long-time friends.

Once Ty stopped the car and ran around to the passenger side, He and his dad supported Sheila, one on each side. She was awake but wobbly as they helped her into the large, tidy house. Before they could get her onto the living room couch, they heard her father's siren. The chief of police did not mess around when it came to his daughter.

He thundered into the room like an angry bear. "What happened?"

Ty respected Chief Williams and was pretty sure it was mutual. He knew the anger was fatherly instinct, and that she shouldn't take it personally. "I gave her a ride home and she passed out."

The anxious father got down on one knee and looked into his daughter's face. She was pale but alert.

"Are you okay, Sugar? What happened?"

"I'm okay, Daddy. I just feel weak."

He stood again and looked intently at Ty, who suddenly realized what it must feel like to be a suspect under the scrutiny of Chief Williams. "Is there anything else you can tell me?"

Ty remembered the letter; he grabbed her purse and pulled it out. "She showed this to me right before she fainted." He opened the letter and handed it to Chief Williams, who read it, then flipped it over to look at the return address. Deep wrinkles etched his forehead. Williams looked inside and pulled out the woven hair. "What's this?"

"I don't know, but she had just pulled it out when she collapsed."

Ty's father stepped up and examined the hair. "This from the mother?"

Chief Williams nodded.

"The voodoo witch doctor lady?"

He nodded again.

Ty was surprised by what his father had said: Voodoo witch doctor lady? Ty knew Sheila's mom had been crazy, but he didn't know she was a witch doctor. He shivered.

"I think we need to get her into your office," Ty's dad said. "Ty, you wait out here."

The older men gently helped Sheila stand and slowly walked her into the chief's office. The door closed in Ty's face.

Ty knew the situation had just gone from being Chief Williams' area of expertise to Reverend Dupree's. He had seen his father take this kind of authority before. He wondered what was going on in there. He pressed his ear against the door but could only hear the gentle tones of his father's voice, not any specific words. Soon the door opened and the three came out. Sheila smiled at him weakly and said, "Thanks, Tyrell, I'll be okay. I'm going up to bed now."

"Thanks, Tyrell," agreed Chief Williams and shook Ty's hand so hard he felt his bones might crack. "We've missed you around here."

"Thanks, Rev," the Chief said to Ty's dad, and the men embraced.

As they walked to the car, Ty was anxious to know what happened. "Dad, what was that about?"

His father turned to him in the failing light, his breath visible in the cold air. "Well, son, there is great evil in the world."

Ty shivered as he remembered the strange look in Sheila's eyes in the car. Evil was a good description. "You mean something evil came into Sheila through that letter?"

His father tilted his head to the left. "Not *in* her, but near enough to try to harm her." He looked at his son and smiled reassuringly. "Don't fret, Tyrell, evil's no match for God. She'll be fine." With that he turned toward his own car and clicked the unlock button. "See you at home."

Ty felt totally unsettled. He'd never given much thought to evil. The closest he'd come to evil was when they had found Dawna in the hands of those sleazy kidnappers last summer, but that was from a distance. This was up close and personal. He shivered, then realized he couldn't feel his toes. He raced to his car. He started the engine and wondered what it would be like to be so sure that evil was no match for God.

Chapter Fifteeen
Darren

"So that's why I can't stay after," said Tiff with a trembling lip. They were at their usual meeting spot by Tiff's locker after school.

Lorna put her hand on Tiff's shoulder. "What about Ty?"

Tiff shook her head, and a tear escaped down her cheek. "I don't know what to do. My mom watches me like a hawk. I haven't even been able to let him know what's going on. My mom took my smart phone and gave me this," she held up a small basic cell phone. "She said it was to save money. I can't even text. I did call Sammy and asked her to have Lando tell Ty, but that's the best I could manage."

"I'm sorry, Tiff. But hey, at least you have a cute new college guy to hang out with."

"I know, but I'm not interested in him that way. I want my Ty!"

"Well, I'd like to meet your cute new college guy," Lorna said with a grin.

"Seriously? Oh my gosh, that would be great. You wanna come with me to the youth group?" Tiff had never thought to invite anyone to her church before. Especially not a white girl, because the services were in Korean, but now there was a youth group in English. Why not?

"Sure, I'll go with you. I used to play guitar in my old youth group."

"Are you kidding me?" Tiff said in awe. Was there anything Lorna couldn't do? "We're having our first planning meeting tonight; do you think you could come?"

Lorna looked happy to be included. "I'm sure I can. You want me to drive?"

"I wonder if my mom would go for that. I'll ask her. She likes you, and it is church. I'll call you after I get home.

∾

MRS. CHO ALLOWED LORNA to drive Tiff and Hanju to the church. The girls chatted happily in the front seat of the Honda Civic while Hanju listened to music and played video games on his phone in the back.

"How come the little prince gets to keep *his* smart phone?" asked Lorna.

"He brought home an A on his English paper. That's the excuse she gave me, anyway."

Lorna glanced in the rearview mirror and said in a soft tone, "Tiff, I heard that voice again."

"What? When?"

"Yesterday. Twice."

"Why didn't you tell me, Lo?" Tiff nicknamed Lorna.

Lorna smiled, "I like that … Lo. It's cute. Well, Tiff, you've been slightly preoccupied."

Tiff felt terrible. She'd been so worried about her own troubles she'd completely forgotten Lorna's. "I'm sorry, Lo. What did you hear?"

"It was pretty creepy, actually. She said, 'I'm coming to get you.' I heard it twice yesterday. Do you think I'm going crazy?"

"Absolutely not. There has to be some other explanation. Did you find out any more about your birth mom?"

"Well," she spoke in the fast clip of a newscaster. "I've wanted to tell you. I actually tracked down the social worker who was in charge of the case."

"No way. What did she say?"

"Well, she wouldn't talk to me. She said it's because I'm not eighteen. I need to have my parents' permission to discuss the case. Since it was an open adoption, she can talk to me once she gets their signed permission. So she sent me the forms and I have to get my folks to sign them in front of a notary, and send them back."

"Will they do it?"

"I hope so; I'm going to corner them on Saturday. I can't wait to get more information."

∾

SUNDAY CAME AND THE small leadership team was ready. Darren seemed thrilled to have Lorna join his group, especially when he found out she played guitar. He, Hanju, and Lorna even had an extra practice with Hanju on the base guitar. Tiff would have felt jealous of their fun if she hadn't let herself get so far behind in her homework she needed the time to cram for a test.

Tiff had no idea what to expect on Sunday. When the meeting started, there were barely as many kids as there were leaders.

They were meeting in some old Sunday school classroom where felt paintings depicting "Jonah and the Whale" and other Bible stories lined the walls.

That's just like the parents to set us up in here, thought Tiff. *They still think we're babies!*

Those who did straggle in, or who were dragged in by their parents, looked as uncomfortable as she felt. Darren put Tiff and Lorna in charge of any younger girls in the group. Their job was to help them feel welcome. Then, during the sharing time, they would break up for discussion in groups with these girls. He and Hanju would do the same with the boys.

As it turned out, there were only three middle-school girls present the first day and no other high-schoolers. Lorna headed straight for two cute sisters who came in with matching outfits. That left Tiff with an awkward girl sitting alone in the corner. She approached her nervously. "Hi, I'm Tiff. What's your name?"

The girl looked up from behind cat-eye glasses. Her hair was parted crookedly but not on purpose, and was held back in white plastic barrettes, the kind a three-year-old would wear.

"Sophie," she said shyly.

Tiff wondered whether the girl could really be in middle school. She looked very young.

Tiff sat down next to her. Earlier, Darren had instructed the group leaders to ask questions and take initiative. Now she could hear him tease the guys in his group, and giggles were coming from Lorna's girls. She shifted in her chair, unsure of what to say. *Come on Tiff, say something!*

"What do you like to do?" she asked with a tight smile.

Sophie started humming, seemingly unaware of Tiff's question.

Tiff glanced around the room, wishing she were anywhere else. *Great, I've ended up with the Korean version of Luna Lovegood!*

"I write songs," said Sophie, startling Tiff.

"You do? Well, that's cool." Tiff felt encouraged. Not many people wrote songs. This was definitely something they could talk about. "What kind of songs?"

"Oh, different kinds, you know. Whatever comes to me."

Tiff did not know. Songs didn't come to her at all. Tennis balls came at her, but that probably wasn't what Sophie was trying to say. She tried for more. "So, where do they come from?"

Sophie pulled off her glasses and cleaned them on the bottom of her blouse. Her eyes, though magnified hugely by the glasses, were actually small and squinted, mole-like, without them.

"Oh, I don't know where they come from. They just arrive. You know, like a package in my head."

Tiff wondered if this was how all people wrote songs. Did they just arrive like a package under the Christmas tree?"

After each answer, their conversation died and Sophie seemed to drift off. *It's like pulling weeds to get this girl to talk.* She tried again. "So, the songs just arrive in your head. Then … you sort of … unpack them?"

"Oh, no!" Sophie laughed loudly, as if Tiff had just said something amazingly funny.

Tiff was shocked at this huge laugh rolling out of such a tiny, awkward girl. But Sophie continued to laugh. She laughed so hard she had to clean her glasses again. Tiff, chuckled uneasily with her and looked around to see if the girl's the hysterical laughter was drawing attention to their conversation. Thankfully, it was not.

Tiff tried again. "So, the songs aren't opened …"

Sophie jumped in, "No, silly, you're so funny! They are downloaded right into my head." Sophie shook her head and chuckled as if she just couldn't get Tiff's joke out of her mind.

"Okay," nodded Tiff, not really understanding. Did all songwriters get lyrics downloaded into their heads?

"Would you like to hear one?"

Tiff's eyes widened. After that loud guffawing she wasn't so sure she wanted to hear Sophie's' song. She chewed on her lower lip. Could she change the subject?

"Here's one I just got today." Sophie began singing in a soft, sweet, childlike voice.

Tiff glanced around to see if anyone had noticed that her charge had just launched into a song. Everyone else seemed busy in their own conversations. *Normal conversations.* Tiff lifted the hair off the back of her neck. Had the heater just kicked into overdrive? Sweat trickled down her back. She tuned into the words Sophie was singing.

"She's coming to get her, the baby she left. She's coming to get her, she feels quite bereft. She's—on—her—way ... to take back the baby she'd given away."

Sophie ended her song and smiled up at Tiff, who sat frozen in stunned silence.

CHAPTER SIXTEEN
LORNA

Lorna gripped the phone harder and paced her bedroom floor as she waited on hold for her social worker to be tracked down. A woman with a thick southern accent came on the line. "Child Welfare, Sandra Jones speakin."

Lorna was caught off guard and stammered, "Hello, uh, this is Lorna Molinari. Uh, I emailed you."

"Yes, Miss Molinari, I received your faxed permission documents today. I'll be glad to talk to you about your case. What is it you wanna know, honey?"

"Well, everything, I guess. Any information you have, that is, about my birth parents."

Lorna heard papers shuffle.

"I can send you a copy of your file, but you need to know it's very slim. Your mother's real name was Wanda Sue Canfield, but she used the alias Debra Jean Miller. She was 27 years old. No father is listed."

Lorna felt herself deflate, like air seeping out of her, taking hope with it. She sat down on her bed. *No father listed. Wanda Sue? Twenty-seven?*

Her childhood fantasy was of a young teenager who had given up her daughter in order to give her a better life. Now she pictured a thin, white woman outside a single-wide trailer, with straggly hair hanging in her eyes and five hungry children clinging to her dress. She realized the social worker was waiting for her to say something.

"Does it say why I was ... taken away?"

"It says here that the environment wasn't safe."

She knew that much, but she wanted more. "But what does that mean?"

"Honey, I can't tell you specifically. It was a long time ago and I'm afraid I've handled hundreds of these cases since then. And, well ... there isn't much information here. I can tell you that in the state of Florida, it's pretty hard to get your children taken away. It generally means there was severe neglect, usually because of mental illness or drug abuse." The social worker said these harsh words as if she'd said them a million times.

Mental illness. Drug abuse. The words hit Lorna like stones. She felt bruised. Still, though, she needed more information. "Is there anything else, like an address or anything?"

"There is a stack of your pictures, sent yearly by your adoptive parents, as per the open adoption agreement. You are a very pretty girl!"

"Um, thanks." Lorna could tell the social worker was trying to give her some kind of hope.

"The pictures were never collected by Wanda Sue ... let's see if there's anything ... oh, looky here, there is an address of the girl's mother on a sticky note."

"The girl's mother?"

"Yes, that would be your grandmother, although the state does try to contact family first for adoption so she could have ... Well, anyway, would you like that address?"

"Yes!" Lorna held her breath. So what if the grandma didn't want to adopt Lorna? She had a grandmother. Maybe Wanda Sue's mom had been too old to take care of a baby. Maybe she couldn't find her. A girl could never have too many grandmas. And if she could find her grandma, maybe she could find her mother ... Wanda Sue.

"Do you have a pen, Darlin'?"

"Yes." Lorna jumped up, ran to her desk and listened intently, scribbling the address. "Sparks, Nevada? Did you say Greenbrae Drive in Sparks, Nevada?"

"That's right, dear. Are you okay? You sound a little ... surprised."

"It's just, that's the next town over from where I live. How did the grandmother get from Florida to Nevada?"

"Probably the same way you did, honey—by moving. Or, it could be the other way around. Maybe Wanda Sue was raised in Sparks and she was the one that moved to Florida."

"I can't believe it!"

"Well, isn't that a hoot! I guess it gives you somewhere to start then, doesn't it? I have no idea how old this address is, mind you."

"Thank you! I'm ... wow, I don't know what to say."

"Well, would you like me to send you a copy of this file?"

"Yes, please, and thank you very much."

"You're welcome; I don't get to do many happy things in my job, so I hope this turns out to be one of them."

Chapter Seventeen
Wanda Sue

"Wanda Sue. Are you kidding me?" Tiff whispered the next day at the lunch table as she dipped fries in copious amounts of ketchup.

"I know," agreed Lorna. "I'm the product of a white trash mother and some loser of a dad who didn't even stay around for my birth!" She pushed lettuce around on her plate with a fork.

"I'm sorry, Lo." Tiff didn't know what else to say. Lorna looked like she hadn't slept much, and Tiff wondered how devastating this news was to her. How would Tiff herself feel if she'd been the one to get this kind of information about her family? Pretty bummed, for sure.

"But I have to tell you the good part," Lorna leaned forward, being sure the rest of the tennis team wasn't listening. "I have a grandmother in Sparks!"

"What? No way!" Tiff bellowed.

"What?" the senior nearest Tiff questioned.

Tiff covered quickly. "Oh, Lorna just told me that she … got a new cable channel.'"

The girl grimaced.

"I've always wanted the … History Channel, you know."

The senior shook her head and turned back to her friends.

"Sorry," whispered Tiff.

Lorna raised her eyebrows in warning. She glanced left to be sure no one was interested in their conversation. "The social worker gave me her address."

"You're not going to contact her, are you?" Tiff thought of the strange song Sophie had sung the other night at the church. She hadn't told Lorna because it had been so bizarre, but she felt it might be a warning for Lorna.

"Well, sure, why not? What have I got to lose? I want to find out what kind of family I came from, and I don't have anywhere else to start. My birth mom never picked up any of the pictures my parents sent in over the years." Lorna looked down at the table.

"I'm sorry, Lo. I'm sure there's some explanation. Maybe she died or something."

Lorna glanced up, worry wrinkling her brow.

Tiff wanted to kick herself. Why was she always stepping on landmines during these conversations? "I mean … well, I'm sure she would have if she could."

"Yeah, I guess."

"But Lo, I don't think you should try to contact your grandma. I mean, these voices you've been hearing are pretty scary. If your mom is trying to contact you … well, she might not be a safe person."

"Yeah, I guess." She picked up a wilted leaf and chewed it slowly.

Tiff could tell Lorna was discouraged, but she was sure of one thing: Contacting Lorna's birth mom was not a good idea. She needed to tell her about Sophie's song.

"Lo, there's something I need to tell you about your birth mom, but not here. Wanna go for a walk?"

Lorna looked up and sighed. Then she grabbed her tray and followed Tiff. They waved to their friends and walked out of the cafeteria. Tiff pulled Lorna into the closest girls' bathroom and quickly checked under the stalls. When she was sure they were alone she spoke rapidly; her voice echoed off the metal walls.

"Did I ever tell you how Ty and I met?"

"You said you met in summer school." Lorna leaned against the wall as if she was exhausted.

"Yeah, well, there's more to it than that. You see, the teacher put us all in groups by the colors of our folders. We were called the Blue Group. We started getting this supernatural information that led us to rescue a girl caught in sex trafficking."

"Wait, what?" Lorna stood up.

Tiff took a deep breath. "Okay, the short version is this. Ty had these dreams, and they gave him information about a certain girl. Then Sammy, who's an artist, drew more information about the same girl. And Lando had these knowings..."

"Wait." Lorna stopped Tiff with her hands up. "You're saying your friends were getting some kind of special information about a girl?"

"Right," Tiff nodded.

"And that girl was a sex slave?"

"Well, it's kind of complicated. But the point right now is ... sometimes people get this sort of supernatural information that can be helpful. It happened again earlier this year with some friends in Loyalton."

Lorna scratched her head. "So, you're saying this information comes from ... where? God?"

"Well, that is the conclusion we came to eventually. There's this verse in Acts 2 that talks about God pouring his spirit out on people, which releases all these gifts. So, it was the best explanation we could come up with, although Ty didn't like it, because he was an atheist."

"Is he still an atheist?"

"I'm not sure. After what happened … well, it was kinda hard to deny that there is a God … so I guess not."

"Tiff, I think it's all really fascinating, and I want to hear more, I do. But why are you telling me about it now? Do you think the voice I'm hearing is from God?"

"Oh, no, not at all." Tiff shook her head adamantly.

"How do you know?"

"I don't think so because the voice you hear is kind of creepy and threatening. But Sophie might be hearing from God."

"Sophie?"

"Do you remember the girl I talked to at the youth group? Remember Sophie, with the glasses?"

"Sure, the funny-looking one? What about her?"

"Well, she makes up songs. She says they just come to her, like they're downloaded into her brain. And … she sang one for me on Sunday. It totally freaked me out."

Lorna stamped her foot. "I'm sorry, Tiff, but this isn't making any sense. What does Sophie's song have to do with my birth mom?"

Tiff grabbed Lorna's arms. "It seems like a warning, and it might be for you."

"Why? What did it say?"

Tiff gulped, pulled off her backpack and took a notebook from her bag.

She read, "She's coming to get her, the baby she left. She's coming to get her, she feels quite bereft. She's on her way, to take back the baby she'd given away."

Lorna's face turned deathly pale.

CHAPTER EIGHTEEN
THE DREAM

Ty woke up in a sweat. It was that dream again. Same white house in the snow, same pull to the window on the left, same creepy figure kneeling before the fireplace, arm raised. How was he ever going to get any sleep with dreams this weird? This time the dream came with a street name: Greenbrae Drive. He knew the street well; it was in Sparks. His family had used to take Roxie, his half-lab/half-basset hound who died two years ago, to her groomer there. He still missed Roxie.

Now he had a house number. But what was he supposed to do with it? He rubbed his eyes and looked at the clock. It was almost time to get up anyway.

It was Wednesday; he had an English test today and could use another half hour to study. English meant Sheila. *I need to check on her anyway.*

He hadn't seen Sheila since the day she had fainted, or whatever it was that she had done. He felt slightly guilty. He was supposed to be her friend, but was always worried about giving her the wrong signals. Since they had English together, he'd have a chance to check on her without having to go out of his way.

He wanted to put the dream out of his mind, and was determined to swing by Wooster and talk to Lando about it after school. Maybe this time Lando would know what to do. Maybe he'd know what to do about Tiff, too.

Ty knew Lando got information about Tiff from Sammy. Maybe he'd heard something new. Tiff hadn't come to their monthly lunch. It would have been their one-month anniversary. He sighed as he thought about it.

He was determined to push both Tiff and the dream from his mind. He had other things to worry about today. Ty rolled out of bed and headed to the shower.

~

"SHEILA, HOLD UP A MINUTE!" Ty called as she left the room surrounded by friends. She turned, smiled, and waited for him. He knew the gossip mill had just received fresh fodder.

"How are you feeling?" he asked when she got close enough to hear. Students bumped him as they pushed past.

"Oh, I'm fine," she said. "Sorry I never got to thank you properly." She rested her hand on his arm. He studied her face, noting the extra makeup she'd put under her eyes. He felt bad for her, and, at the same time, repulsed by her constant over-familiarity.

"No problem," he said, and turned slightly so she had to release him. "Any more weird letters or anything?"

"No, and Dad's got me on a short leash. I have to text him before school, at lunch, and after school," she laughed thinly.

"I'm glad to hear it." He looked at his phone as if to check the time. "Gotta get to class."

"Thanks for your concern. Let's get together soon," her voice trailed after him as he took long strides down the hall.

~

TY BEGAN TO RELAX AS SOON as Lando got in the car. The drive over had been intense; a fresh layer of snow had brought up the eerie feeling of his dream again. It was funny how Lando had a calming effect on him. No one else had that effect on him—well, except maybe his family. And maybe Tiff … but not lately. No, calming was not the effect he associated with Tiff these days.

"Dream again?" asked Lando as soon as he was belted in.

"Yeah." Ty filled him in. "Any idea what I'm supposed to do with this information?"

"No, sorry. Have you heard anything from Tiff?"

"Not a word. I was wondering if you had any news."

Lando's answer was interrupted as they pulled up to the intercom at the Starbucks drive-through. Ty always bought Lando coffee, whether he dropped him at home or took him to Sammy's. He ordered Lando's usual grande mocha with a double shot along with his own caramel macchiato. Today, Lando said he needed to go home. Once they had their drinks in hand, and the car was filled with delicious smells, Ty pointed the Subaru in that direction.

Lando picked up the thread of their conversation. "Sammy says Tiff's really messed up about the whole thing. Her parents have her locked up pretty tight. They took away her smart phone and only let her do homework at the kitchen table so they can monitor her computer."

"But do they even know about me?"

"Sammy says Tiff doesn't think so, but they're suspicious. They even brought this young Korean guy over to get Tiff and Hanju to help lead the youth group at their church."

"How young?" Ty asked suspiciously.

"He's in college. Sammy said Tiff said he was good-looking, too, but she only wants you. Says Lorna is interested in him."

Ty felt flattened by this news. Not only was Tiff inaccessible to him, but now there was competition. How long before she chose the path of least resistance? If she did, would he choose his own easy path—Sheila? He shook his head at the thought. *Never!*

"Ty, don't worry about him, man. She likes you, a lot."

"How am I supposed to date her when we can't even talk? It's so frustrating. I felt like we were finally getting somewhere. It was so good to see her in person at school, ya' know? And now she's not even allowed to come to the Saturday lunches."

"Yeah, I don't know what I'd do if I couldn't see Sammy."

What was wrong with him? Here he'd just whined like a baby and he'd been so preoccupied about Tiff he'd totally neglected his friendship with Lando. "Sorry, dude, how's Sammy?"

Lando's face lit up in one of his famous ear-to-ear smiles. "She's great. The play is almost done and she said the sets look fantastic! You're still gonna come, right?"

"Of course, I wouldn't miss it."

"Sammy says Dawna and her friends from Loyalton will come, too. Maybe I can get my mom and grandma to come."

"How are they, by the way?"

"My mom's okay, but Abuelita … Grandma has the flu. It's a bad one, man, and I'm worried about her."

"Did she get the flu shot?"

"I don't think so; she's convinced they make you sick."

"That's totally unscientific; the viruses are dead before they put them in you."

"Tell that to my abuela."

"Is that why you want to go home today?"

"Yeah, I told Mom I'd be there before she goes to work in case Abuelita needs anything."

Ty pulled up to Lando's duplex. Snow fell in earnest now. "I hope your grandma feels better, Lando."

Before he opened the door, Lando turned to Ty. "Don't worry about it, Ty, Tiff likes you, man."

Ty shook his head solemnly. Liking isn't the problem. He pulled away from the curb. It was one thing to like somebody; it was another if you could never see her. When it came to Tiff, he was going to have to make some decisions.

CHAPTER NINETEEN
YOUTH GROUP

D arren decided to start a Wednesday night youth group as well as the Sunday school class.

Probably my mom's idea, Tiff sighed as she entered the church with Lorna and Hanju. Now they met in one of the bigger classrooms that had been officially designated the new "Youth Room." Rows of chairs were set up in a crescent facing the front, where Darren and his team would lead worship.

Darren was tuning his guitar when they arrived. "Hey, good to see you!" he said as they pulled off coats and scarves. Tiff noticed that Lorna lit up in his presence, and he seemed happy to see her as well. *That's one good thing to come out of this,* Tiff thought.

Lorna and Hanju got out their instruments and started to warm up with Darren. Middle- and high-school kids began to file in. They stomped snow off their boots and unwound fat scarves. Tiff was shocked to see how many came in. At church, there'd been maybe eight kids, but now there were already that many, and the meeting wouldn't even start for another fifteen minutes.

She sat in a chair and watched Lorna and Darren sing together. Lorna wasn't like other girls. She didn't get all flirty or shy around Darren, like so many of the youth group girls did. She was just herself, and "just herself" was plenty. To Tiff, Darren looked positively smitten.

She wondered what her parents would think of that. Had they hoped Tiff would fall for Darren? She felt happy for Lorna and a bit sad for herself at the same time. Would she ever get to see Ty again? Her feelings about him were so mixed up. She hated to deceive her folks and sneak around. It was a huge relief not to do that anymore. She knew her parents just wanted the best for her, but she thought Ty was the best for her. She wanted to be with him without having to lie about it. But she couldn't picture that in this lifetime.

Darren cleared his throat and got Tiff's attention. He pointed his chin toward the door to remind her she should greet, not sit. Grudgingly, she got up and began to wander the room. saying hello to the shy kids who stood around in small clusters. Sophie was back, and the cute sisters, who both had brought friends. Tiff was impressed. She had not even thought to bring Lorna. Lorna had invited herself.

As she mingled, she tried to help the young, insecure kids feel more at home. Her mood began to lift.

Sophie was standing alone in a corner when Tiff approached. "Hey, girl!"

Sophie's smile looked forced. "Hi, Tiff."

Tiff noticed Sophie's wonky hair again and her shirt, which definitely did not match her pants. *Who lets a kid go out looking like that?* "Was that your dad who dropped you off?"

"Yeah, but Darren's giving me a ride home."

"Oh, your dad can't do it?"

"No, he has to work."

"He works at night?"

"Yeah, he's on a night shift at The Peppermill."

"How 'bout your mom?"

Sophie looked down at her shoes. She spoke so quietly that Tiff had to strain to hear her. "She died."

"Oh … I'm sorry. When did that happen?"

"Last summer. Car accident."

"Oh." Tiff felt terrible. Maybe if she'd been more observant she would have caught this earlier and taken more of an interest in Sophie. The poor kid obviously needed some female help. *Maybe if I got my head out of my butt more often, I'd be a nicer person.*

"Hey, Soph," Tiff said, trying out a nickname. "You like to play tennis?"

"I don't know. I've never tried."

"Well, when the weather warms up, how 'bout I teach you?"

Sophie's smile looked genuine this time.

≈

AFTER THE MEETING, LORNA came up and broke the news. "Tiff, I can't give you guys a ride home, but Darren said he would."

"What? Where are you going?" Tiff couldn't think of any reason Lorna would need to dump her on Darren. They didn't live that far from each other.

"I told my mom I'd do some errands for her on the way home." Lorna turned her face away from Tiff. "But Darren said it wouldn't be a problem, so I'll see you tomorrow." Lorna was out the door before Tiff could question her.

Tiff stood there, confusion knitting her brow. What was it about Lorna's expression? Tiff tried to nail it down. *I know! She was lying!* Lorna was a terrible liar. She'd never seen Lorna try to lie before, but that had to be it. Why on earth would Lorna lie to her?

Tiff still pondered the possibilities when Darren came up to her, guitar case in hand. "You ready to go?" He was trailed by Hanju and Sophie. Tiff grabbed her coat as Darren turned off the lights and locked the door.

"Shotgun," Hanju called as they walked slowly through the snow dumped by that day's storm. Stars were now visible through the clearing clouds.

Tiff crawled into the back seat next to Sophie. Her initial reaction to Sophie had softened to a sort of fondness over the last few weeks. She was just an awkward kid with a strange … what? Tiff wasn't sure what to call the singing Sophie did. Was it a gift, like the one of Ty's dreams, Sammy's drawings, or Lando's knowings? Or was it just strangeness?

"Hanju," began Darren, "can you let your mom know we're gonna be a little late? I have to take Sophie home first, and she lives in Sparks. I want to drive really carefully because of the snow, so tell her not to worry if we're late. Tell her I have an all-wheel drive and I'll be careful."

"Got it," Hanju said as he started to text.

Tiff watch his texting capability with envy. What she wouldn't give to be able to text Ty right now. She wondered what he was doing.

～

TY LOOKED OUT HIS BEDROOM window at the snow. It had stopped snowing, but the remaining white drifts glistened under the street lights, lending a magical feel to the night. The buzz of his phone shook him from his reverie. It was Lando.

"What's up?" He looked forward to another chat with his friend.

"Ty, you have to go now."

"Go where? What are you talking about?"

"You have to go to that house in your dream."

"Seriously, Lando? It's freezing and dark out there. I don't want to go."

"I know, and I'm sorry, but I have one of those feelings in my gut, and I can't shake it."

Ty had to trust Lando. Lando's knowings had proven themselves in two dramatic rescues so far. Ty did trust him.

"Then I'll come get you."

"That's the thing, Ty, I can't go with you this time. I have to stay with my abuela."

"Oh." Ty's eye started to twitch. It made sense; no one had been with him in his dream, but the thought of going there alone freaked him out. Who else could he tell that wouldn't think he was crazy? Tiff and Sammy, of course. But he couldn't call Tiff.

"Can I take Sammy?"

"You could, man, but she's at rehearsal."

Ty actually considered his father, but it was Wednesday night and his family was at church.

"You still there?" Lando asked.

"Yeah, man, I'm here. Okay, I'll go."

"Let me know what happens. I'm sorry, Ty. I wish I could go with you."

"I know. I'll let you know." He frowned as he ended the call.

~

DARREN AND HANJU WERE DEEP in conversation in the front, while Tiff and Sophie were playing "Would You Rather" as they rode in the back seat. It was Tiff's turn. "Okay, okay … would you rather jump out of an airplane or … paraglide?"

Sophie shrieked, "Oh, neither, I'm afraid of heights!"

"No, you have to choose."

"Well, then, I choose jumping from an airplane. At least I'd be strapped to someone who knew what they were doing!"

The girls laughed. Tiff actually enjoyed Sophie. She was fine once she loosened up a little.

"Hey, Tiff, wanna hear my new song? Actually, it's the same song; a new verse just came to me."

Before Tiff could protest that she'd prefer jumping from an airplane than hearing more of Sophie's songs, the girl sang, *"She's coming to get her, the baby she left. She's coming to get her, she feels quite bereft. She's—on—her—way … to take back the baby she'd given away."*

"You're singing that song again?" Tiff said. She hoped it would stop her. The tune had already been stuck in her head for days.

"Yeah, and I wrote another verse. Wanna hear it?" Before Tiff could respond, Sophie was singing again, *"She's coming to kill her, the baby she left; she won't take her with her, she feels quite bereft. She's—on—her—way … to kill her baby at 512 Greenbrae."*

"Wait, seriously?" Tiff said. "Did you just sing an address?"

"I don't know. I just sang what came to me."

Darren's voice interrupted them. "We're here, Sophie! See you Sunday."

"Thanks for the ride, Darren. Bye Hanju, bye Tiff!" Sophie jumped out of the car with a happy wave, as if her song hadn't been morbid and strange.

The door slammed and Darren started to pull away from the curb. Tiff couldn't wait to tell Lorna about this one. What would she think of the bizarre song? Suddenly the puzzle pieces fit together in her head. Click, click, click. Lorna lied about where she was going tonight because she was going to see her grandmother, and she knew Tiff didn't want her to. *That's why Lo wouldn't look at me!*

Sophie's song was a warning that Lorna was in big trouble. Hadn't Lorna said her grandmother lived on Greenbrae Drive in Sparks? Sophie's song said something about someone coming to kill ... "Darren, stop the car!"

She had to get Darren to go to 512 Greenbrae Drive, but how? She didn't have time to be creative. She was just going to have to tell him everything.

Chapter Twenty
The Lamb

Ty pulled up to the white house with the picket fence. It looked just like it had in the dream. He sat in the car and looked at the window to his left. There was a dim light in there. A chill ran down his back. What was he supposed to do, just walk up to the door? In the dream, the door had been open and he'd walked inside. What was he thinking? He was a black man, out at night, in a strange neighborhood. He couldn't just walk into someone's house. He'd be shot!

A tap on his window made him jump. He tried to see out, but it had fogged up. Using his gloved hand, he wiped away the condensation. A strawberry-blonde-haired girl was bent down to the window looking in at him. Tiff's friend, Lorna? He opened the door.

"Ty, is that you? I thought I recognized your car. What are you doing here?"

Ty got out and stood next to her. A blast of cold air hit him. "What are *you* doing here?"

"I asked you first."

"Um, well, it's hard to explain …"

"Does it have to do with those dreams you have?"

"Did Tiff tell you about them?" He felt betrayed that Tiff would share something they'd kept to themselves for so long.

"Well, only because ... some kind of weird things have been happening to me, too."

"Like what?"

Before she could answer, a third car pulled up in front of the small house. Darren, Hanju, and Tiff tumbled out and ran toward Lorna.

"Lorna, are you okay?" Tiff wrapped her in a hug, and then she saw Ty, "What are *you* doing here?"

"I could ask you the same question." Ty glowered at Darren, who now stood behind Tiff.

Tiff followed his gaze. "This is Darren, our youth leader. We came because we were afraid Lorna was going to get killed by her birth mother."

"Who's this?" Darren asked, standing taller.

Lorna pushed forward. "What do you mean, killed? How did you even know to where find me?"

"Sophie sang the address when we were taking her home. She sang that you were going to be killed at 512 Greenbrae."

"512? My grandmother's address is 510 Greenbrae." She pointed to the house next to the white one. "I've been in my car. I want to get the courage up to go in, but it's hard. Then Ty pulled up, and I was gonna see if he'd go in with me."

Tiff turned to Ty. "Wait, why you are here?"

Ty kicked at the snow, unsure of what to say in front of Hanju and Darren. "You know the dreams?"

Tiff nodded.

"They led me here, and tonight, Lando ... said it was time to come."

Darren stepped toward the group. "Look, guys, I don't know what's going on, but now that we know Lorna's okay, I think we all need to go home. It's freezing out here!"

Ty said stiffly, "That's fine for you, Darren, but I have to go into that house, and I'd sure appreciate it if some of you would stick around to make sure I come out alive."

Darren looked confused. "I don't understand why you need to go in there? I think ..."

Tiff interrupted, "If Ty says he has to go in, then we all have to go in. That's the way it works."

Ty felt conflicted. He didn't want to go in alone, but he didn't want to endanger anyone else, especially Tiff. The last time they had followed a dream into danger, it had gotten pretty hairy. "No, I'll go in, but could you wait for me?"

Tiff turned and started toward the house. Ty ran to get in front of her. Lorna ran after Tiff and Darren, and Hanju followed. As he got to the small walkway, he heard it again, a blood-curdling scream. The crowd at his heels stopped in their tracks, eyes wide in fear. He turned, grim-faced, toward them and nodded. Taking a breath to calm himself, he turned to the door.

His heart pounded as he walked up the step. Just like in the dream, the door was slightly ajar. He pressed gently and it swung open. It was pitch black and the smell of something spicy sweet was thick in the air. Ty tiptoed into the small hallway and looked to the right. The living room glowed with the light of burning candles. There was the woman he'd seen in his dreams, holding the knife in the air. Something lay at her feet, struggling to be free. It produced a terrible sound.

The group bunched up behind him in the entrance way, craning their necks to see what was happening. Someone clutched him from behind. As Ty's eyes adjusted to the light, he saw the thing that was tied up. It was the size of a dog. *Is she going to kill a dog?*

The woman's skin was deep ebony, glistening with sweat in the flickering light of countless candles.

"What is that?" whispered Tiff.

The woman turned toward them and they jerked back as one, but she didn't seem to see them. She was chanting something in a language Ty didn't recognize. *Maybe she's in a trance. What should I do now?* His dream had stopped here. He knew he needed to go to the room down the hall to the left, but what about the woman with the knife?

Lorna whispered, "We've got to do something, Ty. She's going to kill that lamb."

"What? How do you know?"

"Can't you hear her? She said, 'I offer this lamb to you to whet your appetite, then the girl is your sacrifice.'"

Tiff whispered, "Lorna, she's not speaking English, how do you know what she's saying?"

"Yes, she is. Tiff, that's the voice I've been hearing!"

"What? How can that be? She's not your birth mother."

Suddenly the woman shrieked and the group jerked back. It was the scream Ty had heard in his dream. The thing on the floor bellowed and flailed. It fought against its binding. Ty could see now that it was a lamb, as Lorna had said. A white lamb, with its legs tied together. It was wild with fear. Ty moved forward—he had to stop her.

Her arms held high in the air reached up higher and then plunged the knife down. The room suddenly grew silent and still, like a tableau of a painting. The lamb jerked twice and was still.

Ty jumped toward the lady and his friends followed. She had her back to him, with her hands on the knife, which was still buried in the lamb. He had to get that knife from her. Ty grabbed the woman's hands, which were slick with sweat, and pulled them away from the knife, still stuck in the lamb's body. The sticky sweet smell of copper filled the air as blood poured out of the lamb's chest. Ty's stomach lurched and he clenched his teeth.

The woman came out of her trance and began to fight. She was surprisingly strong. Her hair and body were wrapped in bright African batik cloth. Bangles lined her arms and neck and jangled as she fought. Tiff ran up to help Ty hold her, but the wild-eyed woman shook her off like bug.

Darren jumped in to help. He and Ty each took an arm and held it behind her back. "Stop struggling! We don't want to hurt you!" Ty shouted. The women's eyes jerked rapidly. She continued to fight, screaming unintelligible words.

Ty asked Lorna, "Do you know what she's saying?"

"Yes, can't you understand her? She said 'Don't let them get Sheila, she's my sacrifice.'"

Ty's throat constricted. Sheila? Was she here? Was she okay?

"Sheila?" echoed Tiff.

Ty looked back and forth from the woman to the hall. He had to go.

The woman stopped struggling and they pushed her down on the couch.

"Tiff, call the police. Hanju, you and Lorna hold her down," he yelled. "Darren, follow me."

"But ..." Darren said, looking back at Lorna.

"Fine, you and Lorna, take her. I need one of you to help me."

Lorna and Darren took Ty's place holding the woman, and Hanju followed Ty.

He turned to the darkened hallway and could see the room at the end that had beckoned him in the dream. What was in there? Was it Sheila? Was she okay? The sight of the lamb with the knife in its side came back to him.

He swallowed his fear and walked through the short hall to the door. *Should I knock?*

He turned the door handle. It was unlocked. He pushed the door open. The room smelled sour and wet. He felt Hanju's breath on his neck.

The room was lit only by a naked, weak bulb. Blood streaks marked the dingy white walls. He could see the toilet and sink, but no one was here. His stomach constricted in panic. Where was Sheila? For a moment, he was unable to breathe. Then he heard a moan, from behind the shower curtain. It was her, it had to be her.

He stepped in and pulled back the curtain. Sheila jerked away at the sound, her eyes wide with terror. She lay bound and gagged in the tub, her wooly hair matted with blood, her face swollen and bruised. Her shirt was wet with blood.

Her eyes filled with tears at the sight of Ty. She tried to speak his name around the gag.

"You know her?" asked Hanju.

"Help me get her up."

Hanju stepped into the tub and, with Ty, lifted Shelia. Her legs were shaking and she could not stand. They lowered the toilet seat and moved her onto it.

As Ty untied her gag, Hanju pulled out a pocket knife and started sawing at her bindings.

"You're handy to have around," Ty said.

Hanju nodded, though Ty could see his hands shaking on the rope.

Sheila sobbed as her gag came out, and Ty held her. Blood from her head soaked into his shirt as her body shook against him.

Tiff came down the hallway, cell phone to her ear. "They're almost here. Are you guys okay?" She took one look at Sheila and gasped. Turning away, she said into the phone, "You'd better bring an ambulance, too."

Ty and Hanju supported Sheila as they walked the hallway back to the grizzly scene of the living room. Sheila recoiled at the sight of the woman and flung herself back into Ty's arms.

The crazed woman jumped to her feet, lunging toward the knife again. Darren and Lorna grabbed her, forcing her back onto the couch.

Lorna said, "She says she has to kill her daughter. We have to hold her down."

"Her daughter?" said Ty, the pieces starting to come together in his head. "Oh, Sheila. This is your mother? From Ethiopia?"

Sheila nodded, her head against Ty's chest. "She … grabbed … me after school!" Sheila wailed. "Right after I texted Dad! She hit me hard with something." The girl began to sob again.

"Shh, shh, you're okay now, we have you, and you're safe." He looked over at Tiff and saw a pained expression on her face.

Ty heard the sirens coming. How was he going to explain this? Doors slammed open and police stormed the house like Marines taking a beach. "Freeze! Put your hands in the air!"

Their hands flew up as lights came on and Ty blinked, temporarily blinded.

Sheila's mother lunged for the knife. Officers were on her like flies on butter.

Then all the kids were forced onto the floor and searched. Other officers searched the house. When it was clear no one else was there, the sergeant said, "All right, who can tell us what's happening?"

"I think I can," said Ty.

CHAPTER TWENTY-ONE
GOODBYE

The crazed woman, who ranted when the police arrived, now sat quietly on the couch in handcuffs, head bowed.

Ty still held Sheila tightly with one arm, explaining to the police officers, "This is Sheila Williams, the Sparks police chief's daughter. You need to call him. He's a friend of my family and can explain everything.

"This woman," Ty pointed to the handcuffed woman on the couch who now looked much less frightening in the lighted room, "is her birth mother from Ethiopia. She's been sending threatening letters to Sheila, and today she kidnapped her after school."

The officer interrupted, addressing Sheila. "Is all that true, Miss?" She nodded.

"Johnson, call the chief," barked the officer in charge. He turned back to Ty. "Continue, please."

"When we came in, she killed that sheep," he pointed to the still form near the fireplace, knife still protruding from its side. "And she had Sheila tied up in that bathroom down the hall," he gestured with this chin.

Darren interjected, "He's right, officer."

"And you are ...?" the officer asked.

"I'm Darren Kim. I run a youth group for the Korean church and was just giving these folks a ride home when ..."

Tiff jumped into the conversation, "When we saw Lorna's car. She's in our youth group, so we stopped to talk to her, and that's when we heard the scream and followed Ty into the house.

Darren spoke up. "Officer, I need to get these kids home before their parents freak out. Do you mind if we leave now?"

"Sure, it's too crowded in here, anyway. Just be sure we have all your names and phone numbers before you leave." He turned to Ty and Sheila. "You two need to stay."

Ty knew he could not let Tiff go without some kind of connection. "Officer, do you mind if I walk them out to the car? I'll come right back in." He gently moved Sheila onto a chair as he spoke.

The officer waved Ty toward the front door and turned to the shaken girl. "Miss Williams, can I get you anything?"

Ty and the others hurried outside. They stopped in the front yard, and he noticed the neighborhood was all lit up now. Anxious faces peered out the windows. "I need to thank you all for going in with me," he said with a slight shake in his voice.

Darren nodded, and Ty noticed he held Lorna's hand. Hanju looked like he was in shock, and Tiff still had the injured look he'd seen when Sheila first grabbed onto him. "Darren, can I talk to Tiff a minute?"

Darren handed his car keys to Hanju. "Okay, but hurry it up. Hanju, warm up the car," he directed, "I'll be right there." He pulled Lorna toward her car, and Ty was left with Tiff. He turned toward her and gently took her hands. "Tiff, I think you guys better stick with the story we just told in there, okay?"

"Sure," she said.

"They won't understand about the song," he cautioned.

"I know, but what will you tell them about how *you* got here?"

"I'm not sure yet. But Tiff, there is something I *am* sure about." He looked intently at her as he spoke. "Tiff, I know I love you."

She managed a quavering smile.

He knew he needed to continue before his heart broke in two. "But, the thing is, I can't be around you right now. It's too hard on you, and I hate making you lie to your family. And it's not at all fair to us." Her lips trembled and her eyes fill with tears.

"Is it Sheila?" she asked in a whisper.

"No." He squeezed her hands. "I don't feel that way about her. I never did. It's just, next year is my senior year, and I have to concentrate on school in order to get into Stanford."

"Stanford?" she asked, looking away.

"Yes, it's my first choice. But listen, Tiff," he gently touched her chin and turned her face back to his.

"When you graduate, I'd like us to try again. Do you hear me? Do you understand? I want us to work. It's just not the right time now."

She nodded, and tears spilled down her cheeks. He bent down and kissed her salty lips.

A siren wailed. A police car skidded around the corner, and Ty dropped Tiff's hands. "It's Sheila's dad, I'd better go." He swung around toward the car and walked away, without a look back.

EPILOGUE

Tiff and Hanju waited in the McQueen High School lobby as people began to pour in for the opening night performance of *Man of LaMancha*. Tiff didn't mind having Hanju as her chaperone tonight. Ever since their adventure with Sheila, the siblings were much closer. She had told him about everything that had happened with the Blue Group last summer, and had sworn him to secrecy.

Things with her folks had settled down now that she wasn't working overtime to sneak around behind their backs. She missed Ty desperately, and cried for a week after he broke up with her, but then she realized it all made sense. This just wasn't the right time. Instead, she'd been pouring herself into working with some of the kids in the youth group. Maybe she was beginning to find her purpose; Sophie was starting to blossom.

Tonight would be the first chance she would have to see Ty since that awful night, and her stomach hurt. She glanced down and checked her outfit for the millionth time. She looked great and she knew it. *Well, why not remind him of what he is missing?*

Two familiar faces popped in through the door, and Hanju waved Lorna and Darren over. Lorna glowed as she and Darren approached, their hands clasped.

Tiff was glad for her friend. After that night with Sheila, Darren and Lorna's relationship had cranked up a notch. It had skipped straight from interest to dating. Darren had even gone with Lorna to meet her birth grandmother.

They'd been invited into the small cozy house by the tall woman who was Lorna's grandmother. Lorna said she had been able to see the resemblance immediately, and that it had felt oddly comforting to meet someone she could tell she was related to.

Her grandmother insisted they drink hot tea and eat some cookies before she began her story.

She explained that Wanda Sue had been a drug addict, and had spent her entire pregnancy with Lorna in jail after being arrested for prostituting herself to get drugs. Lorna's father was some anonymous John. But being in jail during the pregnancy meant that Lorna was born clean and healthy, and was promptly removed by Child Protective Services. Lorna's grandma had been heartbroken by the whole thing, and told Lorna how Wanda Sue had been a promising young girl who had started experimenting with drugs in middle school.

Wanda Sue and her mother began fighting regularly until she ran away at the age of sixteen, with an older man she'd met who took her to Florida and then abandoned her. She ended up in a crack house somewhere, and then prison. Wanda Sue was in and out of prison all her life until she died at the age of forty. Her grandmother hadn't known there was a child until after Wanda Sue had died. Then she felt it was too late to contact her, but sent her address to social services just in case the child ever wanted to find her.

Now, as Lorna had shared with Tiff, she met with her grandmother frequently, and sometimes other relatives came over to meet her.

While Tiff had been lost in thought, Lando and Ty had come in. She almost fainted when Ty smiled at her. He had a powerful effect on her that hadn't changed one bit in recent months. Lando was dressed in a suit and carried a bouquet of red roses. His mother and abuela were with him; introductions were made all around.

Lando whooped with delight when Dawna and the Loyalton High group walked in. The friends all exchanged hugs. Dawna had designed the costumes for this show before she had returned home. *Sammy will be so happy to see Dawna,* Tiff realized. They had become very close during the semester Dawna had lived in Reno.

"We'd better go in," Lando said and led the way into the theater. Their group took up a whole row, front and center. Sammy had put their names on the best seats. She came out in the black stage-crew uniform and squealed in delight when she saw Dawna. She received a kiss and flowers from Lando and two kisses each from his mom and grandmother.

Tiff was seated between Hanju and Ty. She felt like she had to hold her breath, unsure as she was about how to deal with being this close to Ty. Right after the lights dimmed, he pushed a note into her hand. She tried to see what was written on the scrap of paper, but it was impossible. The music started, and soon she was caught up on the beautiful story of a man who fights windmills as if they are dragons. The set designs were as perfect as the costumes.

When the lights came up at intermission, Lorna grabbed Tiff's hand to go find a bathroom together. They soon found themselves in a long line of girls and women with the same goal. Tiff reached for the note and raised it just high enough out of her pocket to open it and read it. This was not something she was ready to share. There was only one sentence, written in Ty's blocky script. "I'll be waiting," it read.

ACKNOWLEDGEMENTS

THANK YOU TO CAROL PURROY, my first editor, and Jessica Santina and my other friends at Lucky Bat Books.

Thanks to my critique group from the Unnamed Writer's Group in Reno for your help working out the bugs: Kay Swindle, Jay Leavitt, Ken Beaton, Patty Doty and Forest, and Lucy Lorz and Carol Purroy.

Thanks to my friends who did ethnicity checks: Matt Kim, Morgan Andrews, and Pat Holland Conner. Any mistakes regarding ethnicity are mine alone.

Thanks to my sweeper, Bethany Spanier; my cover artist, Tatiana Fernandez; and my website wonder, Sarah Monahan.

And, as always, thanks to my wonderful family. Without your love and support I would not be writing. David, you are the love of my life and I am so grateful for you.

Thanks to Karl and Pam Shore for the use of their beautiful home when I needed some quiet to edit. Thanks to my Mercy Center friends for offering a monthly retreat.

Thanks to the Giver of Gifts.

Dear Reader

Thank you for following me on the journey through The Birthright Series. I think we are at an end. I have a new book coming out called Bending Willow, which is unrelated to this series, but I'm very excited about it. After that, who knows? Maybe I'll find our friends Ty, Tiff, Sammy, and Lando as they reach college and need to have more adventures. Keep posted and we'll see what happens.

Abduction of children by strangers is not the only kind. Parental child abduction is a large and growing problem. For more information on children abducted by parents, go to www.globalmissing.com

As always, you can reach me through my website at jacciturner.com or email me at Jacci@jacciturner.com. You can also find me on Facebook.

Much love and joy … dream on!

Jacci

ABOUT THE AUTHOR

JACCI LIVES IN RENO, NEVADA with her husband, David, and a sweet, big, yellow dog. Oh, and the whitewashed memory of the perfect cat.

Jacci loves to read and write and spend time with people half her age, feeling generally hopeful about the world.

She enjoys chocolate in all of its manifestations.

"I began writing The Birthright Series three years ago. The first book took me a year to write. I wrote a chapter every Tuesday, and after a year, the book was done. Then two years, sixteen edits, and fifty rejections later, I'm published! Piece of cake!

BOOKS BY JACCI TURNER

The Birthright Series

The Cage
The Bar
The Lamb

Made in the USA
Charleston, SC
05 December 2012